El Roi

God Who Sees Me

Jo Wanmer

El Roi — God who sees me
© Jo Wanmer 2025

Published by Armour Books
P. O. Box 492, Corinda QLD 4075 Australia

Cover Images: imamember | iStock: Portrait of a young man
  with curly hair; Bhavesh Patel | Unsplash;
  Whimsy Girl | Creative Fabrica
Interior: Jacpot07 | Creative Fabrica; Dustin Humes | Unsplash

Cover design, interior design and typeset by Beckon Creative

ISBN paperback: 978-1-925380-95-8
ISBN ebook: 978-1-925380-96-5

A catalogue record for this book is available from the National Library of Australia

All rights reserved. No part of this publication may be reproduced, stored in, or introduced into a retrieval system, or transmitted, in any form, or by any means (electronic, mechanical, photocopying, recording or otherwise) without the prior written permission of the publisher.
Note: Australian spelling and grammar conventions are used throughout this book.

. . .

After her encounter with Yahweh,
Hagar called him by a special name,
'You are the God of My Seeing,' for she said,
'Oh my, did I just see God and live to talk about it?'

Genesis 16:13 TPT

. . .

Acknowledgements

I AM A STORY TELLER more than a polished writer. I want to thank all those who have laboured over this manuscript to polish it ready for publication. A special thank you to my good friend, Sue Ford, who has patiently edited this work countless times. I'm deeply indebted to her. Her encouragement has fuelled me to the finish line.

Thanks also to the community of writers at Omega Writers, who have taught me how to write a good story. They gave me an Encouragement Award in the CALEB awards two years ago. That encouragement and another prophetic word gave me a big enough push to pick up the pen again. I'm so glad I did.

Thanks also to Jeanette Grant-Thomson who edited the manuscript and Arlene Dodson who sniffed out countless mistakes.

To Anne Hamilton of Armour Books—without your faith in me, my books would still be languishing on my computer. I'm indebted to you.

Contents

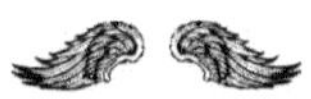

Introduction

EL ROI IS A PREQUEL to *El Shaddai* and the other books in the series. When I finished *El Shaddai*, Dan's character demanded his story be told. We didn't see a lot of Dan in *El Shaddai* even though he was an important part of the story. A man of great faith, he wanted the beginnings of his faith to be explained, so I explored his earlier life. Now I'm pleased to share it with you.

This is a read alone book, as is *El Shaddai*, but the two read together add richness to each other. I hope you enjoy Dan's journey.

Chapter 1

HOLDING THE BLADE STEADY, he made a long vertical slash… not too deep, but enough to extract a few pages from the book. He spread three pages out on his desk. *Psalm 2.* The words jumped from the page.

Sorry, Gran. He shook the thought away. He needed to focus… and thinking about Gran's gift of the little red Bible wasn't going to help. Turning back to his task, his eyes watered and blurred the edges of the paper. He focused his attention on extracting more tobacco. Some of it had come into his possession when Dad left his pouch unattended. Raiding the bin of the binge smoker in one of the other units gave him the rest. He dismantled another butt and dropped the smelly brown flakes into a saucer. When he had enough, he would mix it with the marijuana he'd bought this morning.

How had he ended up here, dealing in drugs? He pushed his fist against the sharp pain throbbing in his heart. It felt like shattered dreams…

He'd had great dreams… *still* had great dreams. But he had to matriculate, get an entrance to university. Schools needed money, he realised that. Dad refused to help. Love it or hate it, this was the only way he could think of.

He'd always dreamed his dreams with Gran… together they'd made his great plans to be an engineer. They'd sit with biscuits and a glass of milk and together they'd plan. She always said he could do anything he wanted to—if he set his mind to it. First step was study hard at school. *Done.* Ticked that box. Second step was university and then find a good firm to work for, to continue learning. But she'd gone. Just like that, her aging heart had said 'enough.'

And now Mum was gone too. Not that she'd died, but it might be easier if she had. He'd come home from school one day and she and his little sisters had disappeared. If she'd left a note, Dad must have taken it. He was in a feral mood so Dan decided to make himself scarce and escaped for the afternoon. When he got home, his father was out, probably drinking.

Dan shook his head. His heart hurt every time he thought of his mum. But he was fifteen. Big enough to look after himself, Dad said. And he was. But he needed money. So he'd borrowed one joint, turned it into three and sold a new product. *Bible Minis.*

He mixed the hash with the tobacco, divided it between the three papers and rolled. Dan's tongue licked the edge of *Psalm 2* and pressed the papers together. Holding it up to the light that slanted between the faded, dirty brown curtains he checked his construction. Yup. It sealed well. The three rolled cylinders dropped into a flip-top carton. The butterscotch sweets settled back in the box hiding its precious cargo and masking its odour... mostly.

El Roi

If he sold all of them tomorrow, he'd have enough cash to buy new school shorts and be back in school on Monday. Being in school was essential for doing well—for getting to uni.

Sealing the remaining bit of his product in the tin marked *Ready Remedy*, he grinned at the irony. Gran would be disappointed if she knew he was using her old tin to store his drug stash. But it was a remedy for sure. Her way of helping to reach his goals. Today he'd paid for the borrowed smoke and bought more stock. Now everything else he sold was pure profit. He did a quick calculation. The smokes in the tin would pay for sports shoes as well as the shorts and maybe a few other important things a bloke needed like milkshakes and footy tickets. Or even two movie tickets if...

He shook his head. She wouldn't be interested. Better he bought new shorts so he didn't miss too much school. A hot flush ran up his neck as he remembered his pants exploding while he did the squats in front of his whole sports class. It wouldn't have been as bad if his dacks hadn't had holes.

Get over it, Dan. He pushed his blonde hair out of his eyes and yanked out the top drawer of the cabinet. Three pieces of balled Blu-Tack held his tin secure on the roof of a crevice between the top of the cabinet and the first drawer. No one could see it there. He could only feel it. Satisfied, he picked up the drawer to replace it and paused. The Bible, little and red, lay open on the bed, the blade beside it. His dad would be furious if he discovered he'd cut pages out of his Bible. Not that Dad ever read the Bible. He left that to Mum.

But Mum was gone. *Sorry, Mum, but desperate times call for desperate methods.* He could almost hear her voice. *Tough times don't last, Dan, but tough people do.* A rubber band and a bit more Blu-Tack would do it. Putting the blade in the Bible, he secured it with the band and slid the tin, moving it to the edge of the crevice and making way for its partner in crime.

Dan slammed the drawer shut, but instead of a satisfying bang it bounced back. With his left hand he pushed the drawer again. Pain shot down his arm.

A car roared into the drive and squealed to a stop. Dan shoved the drawer in place with his hip, pushing down the mess of socks and jocks with his right hand.

Swallowing tears, he zipped the box of sweets in an inner pocket of his backpack. A car door slammed. He'd determined never to cry again…

The front door banged open. 'Dan!'

When he was younger he would have hidden in his cupboard. Not that it worked for long. His Dad always found him. Now his lanky frame couldn't be hidden by a cupboard, the only protection he had was agility and speed.

A steel-capped boot kicked the bedroom door open. It belted into the wall, the handle plugging the hole in the plaster caused by many similar events. His father's fists were balled and the vein on the left side of his neck bulged. 'Why aren't you at school?'

'Maybe cos I'm not welcome without pants?' Dan backed around the bed. If his father followed he might be able to jump the bed and run.

'I fixed those duds for you.' The flare in his eyes made Dan swallow his caustic return.

'S…sorry. I forgot. I'll be in school tomorrow.'

His father stopped at the corner of the bed. 'Forgot! I'll give you "forgot". I use up my precious time to staple your

El Roi

pants good and you... you *forget*.' He clenched and unclenched his fist. 'Then I get a call from some snivel-nosed busybody at the school. As if I need anyone to tell me how to raise my own kid!' As a tiger eyes its prey, he fixed his dilated pupils on Dan and with measured steps advanced for the kill.

Jump the bed and run. He could… but he couldn't. There was enough room, but black eyes captured him, and he shook helpless as the aggressor advanced. 'I'm sorry, Daddy. I'm sorry.' He twisted as the first punch hit his left shoulder.

Chapter 2

'Dan Furley!'

'Yes, Sir.' Dan shoved his hand through his hair and held it off his face, hoping his hand hid the bluish, yellow bruise.

'Mr Blueberry wants to see you.'

'Okay, Sir.' His stomach dropped. What did Bluey want with him? And what if he asked about the black eye? He'd packed frozen peas on it all weekend, hoping it would disappear.

'*Now*, Furley.'

'Now, Sir?' He scraped back his chair and gathered his books, dropping his hair to cover his eyes. Halfway across the quadrangle his heart skipped a beat. Two rollies lay in his shirt pocket, not even concealed in a folded tissue, his planned precaution when he took them from the lolly box. The toilet block? Too obvious if anyone was watching. *Think, Dan, think or you're dead meat.*

He bent, faking a coughing fit and slipped the cylinders from his top pocket into his clenched fist, then shoved them in his pants pocket.

The Administration block was only a few metres away. His pulse raced but his stride didn't falter. One thing he had learned from his father—how to hide fear. His thoughts raced back to the beating the other night. He'd caved into fear then. *Never again.*

Pushing open the glass door his eyes scanned for a place to drop his valuable cargo. A bin? A pot plant? But he'd never get them back and he had boys expecting them at lunch. Three more steps and he'd be in front of the closed door. Of course. Above Bluey's door. His right hand slid the evidence onto the narrow ledge. His left hand tapped under the sign, *B B Blueberry, Deputy Principal.*

'Yes?'

Wiping his sweaty palms on his new shorts, he swung the door wide. 'Dan Furley, Sir. You sent for me?'

Bluey waved him to a chair. 'Dan, meet Mrs Rhodes, our new student counsellor.'

Dan moved toward the petite woman and held out his hand, careful not to lift his head too high. 'Welcome to Nundah High, Mrs Rhodes.' It wasn't normal for a kid his age to shake a teacher's hand. But he had to make a good impression. Student Counsellors were to be cultivated. She could help him reach his goals. Standing, she accepted his offered hand. *Soft.* It was the only word to describe her. Her hand, her hair, her eyes and the sweet aroma of flowers drew him.

He dropped her hand and steeled his heart. She'd be easy to manipulate, to make sure he got the subjects he wanted and special dispensation here and there. He dared not let his heart be drawn in.

 El Roi

Bluey stood and came around his desk. 'Dan, I believe you have a face injury?'

'Sir?' His heart sank. He should have stayed home one more day but Monday's classes were important to him. New ideas were taught, assignments were set and hangovers helped sales.

'May I?' With one finger Mrs Soft lifted his blond camouflage. Her eyes dropped lower and looked at his jaw. She glanced at Blueberry.

'It's nothing, Sir, Miss. I was doing sit ups and lifted the pace, not realising the bed was so close. My room's only small, you see, and my bum must have been moving forward and I didn't realise it.' His own voice rattled in his ears as though he had ADHD and was on steroids.

'And the neck?' She rose on tiptoes and peered at his shoulder. He hadn't applied as much ice to his shoulders and neck. With only two bags of frozen peas he'd chosen to concentrate on the exposed spots.

'Got into a fight at the park on the weekend...' He was running out of good ideas.

'Have any of these injuries been checked by a doctor?'

'No, Miss. They're fine.'

'I'd like to take you to ER and get a doctor to make sure nothing is broken.' Soft brown eyes met his, eyes reminiscent of his mother, except Mum's were always full of pain—deep, deep pain.

'Thanks, Mrs Rhodes, but it won't be necessary.'

'I think it's necessary.'

'I'll get Dad to check it out tonight.'

A siren signalled the classes were changing. He grabbed the audible lifeline. 'Would you excuse me, Sir? My maths class is about to begin. It's hard to catch up if you miss the beginning.'

Bluey looked at Mrs Soft.

She sighed. 'Thanks, Dan. I'll need a medical certificate about your injuries. Shut the door as you leave.'

The door clicked behind him. He raced to his classroom, his hidden cargo forgotten.

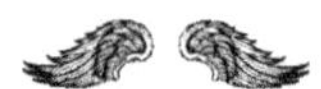

THAT NIGHT, THE EMPTY BAKED beans tin missed the bin in the corner and rolled under the table. Dan muttered a swear word. He never missed. Well, hardly ever. He blinked a few times trying to focus his vision. Double vision had plagued him a few times after Dad had got really mad, but it cleared in a few days. It would be fine in another day or two. And it was his own fault. He'd forgotten to ring the school and report in sick. Since his mother had gone, it was part of his responsibilities; like signing permission slips, getting his own dinner, even cleaning the bathroom after the results of Dad's binge drinking hit the floor and the walls instead of going in the pedestal.

He flicked up the pull-ring on the second can of beans and shovelled them into his mouth with a fork. His mum wouldn't be happy he was eating out of the can, but cans didn't have to be washed up and she wasn't here. He swiped angrily at a tear that escaped from the corner of his eye. *Toughen up, Dan.*

He ripped an A4 sheet of paper in half, using his ruler. No way was he wasting a whole sheet on a stupid school note.

 El Roi

'To Mrs Rhodes. I have taken Dan to the medical centre. There is nothing broken.'

He signed it 'Alf Furley'. The signature he'd practiced for weeks now flowed from his pen. The folded note was shoved in his pencil case. The second tin missed the bin and rolled towards the sink leaving a trail of tomato sauce. He lifted his right hand to pound the table but stopped. He couldn't afford to hurt his writing hand.

He pulled out his maths homework. The new concepts today fascinated him, but he hadn't quite understood. He would understand it in class tomorrow but not before Nerdy Neil had shown off his superior knowledge. Neil always understood because his father was an engineer. And he talked to him. And he helped him. And bought him a laptop and a phone. *Suck it up, Dan. Who needs a father anyway?*

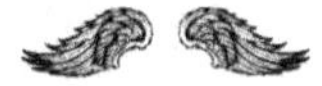

RUNNING LATE, DAN RACED down the ramp next morning and swiped his card as the train approached. The machine declared he had five dollars credit. Dad was on his phone last night so must have topped it up. Life was much easier when he didn't have to dodge ticket-checking dudes. He ran beside the train to get to the second last carriage. She always sat in the same place. Through the door he pushed past a couple of suit-clad businessmen hanging onto the silver rail. The train started to move as he jumped a pile of school bags.

There she was. His heart did a happy dance as he closed the gap.

'Hey.' The train jerked, throwing him toward her. A frantic grab at an overhead strap stopped him landing in her lap.

'Thanks for dropping by.' Her green eyes sparkled under chocolate bangs. 'I was beginning to think you'd dumped me.'

They travelled the same train together, for four stops, every day. These were the golden minutes of his existence. But there were other carriages to hide in when he preferred not to expose her to his busted pants and black eye.

'Business has been keeping me busy.' He squatted on his backpack beside her seat, resisting the urge to hug her. Instead lay his hand palm up on his knee and wiggled his fingers, offering, hoping, waiting.

'Business?' She ran one nail across his fingers. A shiver ran the length of his spine.

'Got to build enough business to be able to impress your Daddy.'

'What's my father got to do with it?' She dropped her hand on his. As his fingers closed over the soft flesh, his mouth ran like water rushing downhill.

'One day, my beautiful Amalya, I'm going to have a good job and enough money to knock on your front door and ask him ...' The train screeched to a stop and kids pushed in, jockeying for places to stand. Behind them an older lady with a stick struggled on the train, eyes searching for a seat. Dan jumped up and grabbed her hand. It wasn't soft, but rough and cracked. The old fingers clung to him as the train lurched forward.

Amalya stood and he lowered the woman into her seat. With backpacks at their feet, they clung to leather straps hanging from the ceiling. He risked throwing his arm around her shoulders. In all the months they'd sat together, he'd never dared such a move.

El Roi

She stood taller than he expected, only a little shorter than him. His whole body tingled as they swayed together with the train. His mouth had gone dry and his brain was empty. *Talk, man. Say something clever.* Her clean fresh smell filled his nostrils.

'I've missed you, Dan.' She stretched her mouth to his ear. 'This train is hell when you're not on it.'

'I'm sure there are other guys wanting to keep you company. I've seen them eyeing you. No wonder.'

'What?' She pulled back and looked at him.

The train lurched to a stop and more kids pushed in as though there was only one carriage on this whole train. Static preceded the announcement, 'Next stop Nundah.'

Half the carriage would empty with him. If he stayed he'd have two more stops with her. It was tempting, but then he'd be late.

She lifted her mouth to his ear; the soft puff of air stood every hair to attention. 'Ask Daddy what?'

'What?'

'You said you would knock on my door and ask Daddy...?

His heart pounded. His fingers squeezed her shoulder, pulling her closer. The train brakes squealed as they slowed for his station.

'Tell me, Dan. What do you want to ask my father? For a job?' Light brown flecks danced in her eyes. She smelt clean and fresh. The carriage jolted to a halt.

'If I can marry you.'

His school mates shoved past him. Her eyebrows shot up under her hair. Without thinking, he dropped a kiss on her head, grabbed his backpack and ran for the door, jumping off as the doors started to close. He turned to see her but she was gone, carried away to her posh private school. He groaned. Who did he think he was?

El Roi

Chapter 3

Doodles covered his page as the English teacher droned on. 'Dan.'

He snapped to attention, crumpling his paper in a ball. No one could see *Dan & Amalya Furley* written in every shape and size. Heat raced up his neck as he stood. 'Yes, Miss.'

'The office called. They want you there now. I didn't know you were leaving today. I'm sorry.'

Dan shook Amalya's green eyes and her chocolate hair out of his fuzzy mind. 'Pardon, Miss?'

'The office...'

'Did you say... *leaving?* I'm not leaving.'

'I hope I'm confused. Why don't you go to the office and see what they want.'

Fear boiled in his belly as he strode from the room, every eye on him. Not another school, not now when he was so close. When he'd worked so hard.

For the second time this week he pushed open the glass doors, ignoring his own angry face glaring at him from the reflected glass. It disappeared as the door opened for him. 'You want me?'

'Dan Furley?'

He bit down the rude retort and made himself nod.

'We need you to sign these transfer papers. Normally they are signed by a parent but your father doesn't have time to come in.' She pushed four pages across the desk and offered him a pen. 'Your Dad has supplied the details. Just sign at the crosses.'

'Transfer?' his voice wavered. A fury swirled in the bottom of his belly. A beating he could handle. A few days of pain and things were back to normal. But this? This stole his entire future, every hope he had. 'To where?' His voice squeaked as if he was fourteen, not nearly sixteen.

'As you're going on the road, you're transferring to the Correspondence School.'

'No.' The fury exploded within. He knew how to control his tongue but his fists balled the forms and threw them across the room. He fell to his knees and covered his head with his arms. Pain flowed in trickling tears across the tiles. 'No, Daddy. I'm sorry, I'm sorry.'

A small form knelt in front of him. 'Dan, shhh. It's all right.' Mrs Rhodes stood and beckoned. 'Please come with me. Just a few steps. We'll go in here.'

His feet dragged. His legs shook. He stumbled down the hall and through the door marked 'B B Blueberry.' All he could think was he wanted to smoke those rolled minis that still lay above the door.

Mrs Rhodes put a bunch of tissues into his hand and led him to a chair. Sitting beside him, she waited in silence but

El Roi

her empathy flowed over him. Emotions warred within him. Embarrassment and devastation fought with his anger. He needed an escape plan but his mind pumped out hopelessness. A spot to the side of his left temple pulsed and seemed to rattle his brain. Someone placed a glass of water on the desk where he could reach it. He grabbed it, swallowing with great gulps.

'They won't be long, Rose.' It sounded like Blueberry, but the door clicked closed before he could turn.

The smokes. He longed for the oblivion they offered… or he hoped they offered. He'd never put one between his lips because protecting his brain was important. His big plans meant he couldn't afford to play around. 'I only did it for cash. I needed the cash for school.'

'What did you say, Dan?' Mrs Rhodes leant closer, trying to hear.

Did I say that aloud? Groaning, he lay his head on the desk and tried to think. He lifted his head and turned toward Mrs Rhodes. 'Is there any other way?'

She was his student counsellor. She must know.

'Is there any way I can stay? Have I got to stay with Dad? I want to finish school, I must finish school. I promised Gran. I can look after myself. I'll…' The words froze on his lips as his father's voice assaulted him through the closed door.

'I told you I was leaving at 2 pm. Where is he?'

Mrs Rhodes put one finger to her lips and shook her head.

'Why isn't the paperwork ready?' A fist hit the counter. 'Just get Dan and forget the paperwork. He's old enough to work and I'll need him for this contract.'

One part of Dan wanted to run to his father before he got too angry. The other wanted to hide. Mrs Rhodes stood between him and the door, blocking his escape route.

'I never want to see the bastard again.' He hissed the words at the gentle face.

Her eyes held his. 'I'm trying, Dan, I'm trying.'

'Mr Furley!' The headmaster's voice filtered through the wall. 'Please come to my office. The paperwork won't be long.'

Fear gained the upper hand in Dan's muddled head. He jumped to his feet. 'I ... I have to go.'

'No. Sit down, Dan.' Her schoolteacher voice stopped him. 'First, we have to sort a few things. I intend to do all I can to help you finish and qualify for university.' She turned at a soft tap on the door. 'Yes?'

Blueberry ushered in two men: men he'd never seen before. Dan glared at them. *Who are they?* A shudder of fear ran up his spine. *What's going on?*

The taller of the men shoved his hand out. 'Dan, my name's James. My colleague is Rodger.' Dan took the offered hand. His handshake was weaker than Mrs Rhodes's soft fingers. The second man just nodded, black sunglasses slipping off his head.

James introduced himself to the counsellor and waved Dan back to his chair. Mrs Rhodes turned her gaze from Dan to the men and waited. In the silence Dan blew his nose, balled the wad of tissues and pitched them toward the bin. They hit the outside of the bin and fell in a sodden mass on the floor.

Mrs Rhodes's soft, vice-like voice stopped him from retrieving them. 'They're fine, Dan.'

James coughed behind his hand. 'Um, Ben ...'

El Roi

'Dan,' the counsellor corrected them. Something in Dan wanted to hug her. She was a goodie.

'Oh, yes. Dan. We're from Family Services and have come to make sure it's within the guidelines of the law for your father to remove you from your education with no notice.' He paused and looked around the room as if trying to find a sign to read, or a hole to fall into. 'We also have reports of untreated injuries.'

'There's a letter covering that. I dropped it at the office yesterday… for Dad.' Dan crossed his arms over his chest so his right arm could support his aching left shoulder and put pressure on his churning stomach.

'We need a medical certificate from a doctor, I'm afraid. Rodger here is going to take you to a medical clinic at Albion. I will be talking to your father regarding your sudden withdrawal from school.'

Rodger pushed his sunnies up over his hair. 'Ok, Dan. Let's go. We have an appointment to keep.'

'My mum told me never to get in a car with strangers.' He hugged his belly tighter, tucking his shaking fingers under his arms.

James stood and left the room. Rodger held out a hand. 'Come, Dan. This way.'

Dan turned to Mrs Rhodes. Her hands lay in her lap, bright pink nails picking at a thread. 'Did you snitch on me? I thought you were helping me.'

Startled eyes met his. 'Dan. I *am* helping you.' The soft hand reached toward him. 'Would you like me to come with you to see a doctor?'

'I'm not a baby.' Indignation flooded his neck.

'A baby? Goodness, no, you are the greatest gentleman I've met on this campus.' She looked at his folded arms as though she could see the pain. 'But I don't want to risk permanent damage to this arm. May I?' Taking his left hand in hers she walked toward the door. He followed. Her grip was definite. To resist and put pressure on his shoulder was unthinkable. He followed, confused, frustrated and willing his stomach to behave.

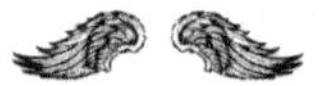

'HOLD STILL.' There was a click and a buzzing sound and the young woman rushed back into the room. She lifted the X-ray machine, pushing it toward the white tiled ceiling. 'Just hang in here a sec, till I check I've done enough slides.' With a grin she disappeared through the back door.

He stayed on the hard bed, head on the pillow counting holes in the tiles. Nineteen per row, twenty-three rows per tile. Anything but face his circumstances, think about what could happen next. Maybe he'd just stay on this bed.

'Dan. We're done. Good clear pictures. My boss is happy, so thank you for being a great patient.' She stood waiting with the stupid sling in her hands. She was a looker but not a touch on Amalya.

He swung his legs to the floor and allowed her to position the sling. 'Thanks.'

The wardsman waited outside the door with the wheelchair. Dan had refused to get in it at first, but they assured him it was protocol. Not a way to stop him escaping. He sat like a trussed-up zombie as walls rushed past, lift doors opened and they followed the green line through emergency.

El Roi

Mrs Rhodes waited in a chair beside his empty bed. Rodger was nowhere to be seen. A baby screamed through the curtain.

'How'd it go?' Her caring eyes watched him sit on the bed.

He shrugged. 'Clear pictures, she said. Mrs Rhodes, what do these men want with me?'

'They are only trying to make sure everything is okay. I believe James was going to suggest your father didn't remove you from the school. He was going to ask him to let you stay until your education is complete.'

'As if. Dad doesn't care about education. Says it's for sissies and rogues like solicitors.'

'You're neither a sissy nor a solicitor, Dan. What would you like to study?'

'Engineering. But Dad wants me to be a plumber or a bricklayer so we can build houses together. Engineering is just another form of building, but he calls them interfering poofters.'

'Engineering is a very exacting profession. I'd be very proud if a son of mine became an engineer.'

He turned his head and swallowed the tears. He must stop crying. And fighting against the inevitable. This was like the beltings. It didn't matter what he did, they always happened. Leaving school was happening. He may as well just accept it. Who was he to think he could be anything more than his dad's lackey?

'Dan.' She leaned closer, eyes intense. 'Dan never, never let go of your dreams. Sometimes they are delayed or even derailed. But if you hang on to the dream, regardless of what happens, it will come to pass.'

When Rodger returned, he offered Dan a can of Coke. A small woman marched in after Rodger. A stethoscope hung from her neck and a wad of cards flapped from her belt. 'Hi, Dan. I'm Doctor Alice McGunn. I'm afraid your collar bone is broken... more than once. Can you tell me what happened?'

'Happened?' Dan mind raced. What story had he told Mrs Rhodes? He couldn't remember.

'Yes.' The doctor sat on the edge of the bed. 'How did you get the injury?'

'Just a scuffle with a few guys at the end of last week. I can't remember much about it.'

'Do you have problems with your memory?'

'No. I learn quickly.'

'What about your eyesight?'

Dan bit his bottom lip. Everything felt unsafe. 'My eyesight?' He felt like a cracked record.

'Hard to read? Blurry vision? Squinting to see the television?'

'It goes blurry now and then.'

'Was it like that before the blow to your head?'

'Sometimes.'

'After previous blows to the head?'

'Sometimes.'

She turned to a tall skinny guy beside her. 'I'll need an eye specialist and an MRI. Run a full set of bloods and strap the shoulder.' She turned her attention to Rodger. 'I think it best to hold him overnight to allow the tests to happen. Tomorrow we will have a clearer picture.'

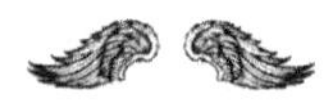

El Roi

Rodger led the way through the car park, Dan's backpack over his shoulder. 'Does it feel good to be discharged?'

Dan kicked a coke can from one foot to the other, his left arm trussed like a chook ready to be cooked. *A chook.* He could relate. Naked, exposed, powerless and heading toward hot water. There had been no word from his father. Either he'd abandoned Dan or he was about to get the biggest thrashing of his life. He hoped he'd been abandoned.

'This is our car.' Rodger waved to the passenger's door, threw Dan's bag on the back seat and climbed behind the wheel.

Dan struggled to handle his seat belt with one hand. Another week of having only one arm. He wiggled his fingers on his left hand. At least they worked a bit. Rodger turned to help with his belt.

Dan glared at him. 'I can do it. I'm not useless, you know.' He decided on the truth. 'And no, it doesn't feel good to be discharged. I'm still a prisoner.'

'You're not a prisoner, Dan.'

'Not feeling free, man. I don't even know where you're taking me.'

Rodger left the car park and turned into the traffic. 'How about we stop at Maccas? We can eat and talk. I'll try and explain.'

'Whatever.' Dan glared out the window but his stomach leapt at the thought of food. Most of the hospital food was cardboard with less taste than baked beans. 'Does it have decent coffee?'

'You drink coffee?'

'Yeah. I love coffee.'

'Then I know a place that does great coffee and bacon and egg sandwiches. Will we try there?'

'Cappuccino?'

'Coming up.' Rodger grinned. 'We're out of hospital quicker than I anticipated so we've got a bit of time.' He swung the car onto a ramp leading to the freeway. 'Coffee by the beach.'

The beach? Fear turned his stomach. What would Dad say if he found out he'd been wasting time at the beach? 'What about Dad? Is he expecting me?'

'Not today.'

Dan relaxed in his seat. 'Okay. If you're not kidnapping me, I'd love to see the beach.'

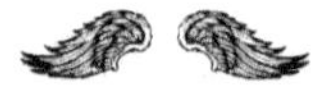

WATER. THERE WAS WATER everywhere, on both sides of the car. Yet the freeway continued, three lanes wide.

Rodger changed to the left lane. 'Ever been here before, Dan?'

Dan shook his head, causing pain to spike his neck and shoulder. 'Where does it go?'

'It's a long bridge but it crosses the mouth of the Pine River.'

'Looks like the sea to me.'

'Yes. The tide is high. When the tide is out it looks more like sand banks.'

Dan watched three huge birds fly toward them. They looked so heavy it was amazing they could stay in the air. They lifted giant wings and settled on top of the streetlights.

Rodger changed back to the middle lane. 'Don't trust pelicans. One pooped on my windscreen once. Couldn't see

 El Roi

a thing. I shoved on the wipers. Bad mistake—it just spread it everywhere. Tried the washers. They were empty.'

'What'd you do?'

'Stuck my head out the window—then I got an eye full.'

A chuckle stirred in Dan's belly and pushed its way upward. He found himself laughing out loud.

'So… I'm driving with one hand, trying to get poo out of one eye with the other hand. My good eye is peering through a stripe of yellow-green slime. I prayed a cattle truck would come past and wash my screen with cow pee.'

Dan was still laughing when they pulled up beside the ocean. Blue water curled white on yellow sand. He crossed the footpath and walked onto grey plants that reminded him of sparse unmown grass. Birds swooped and called. The wind in his face tasted like salt and smelt like the prawn heads Dad dumped in the bin behind Coles.

'Take your shoes off, mate, and go for a walk. I'll go and get the food.' Rodger headed across the road.

Dan spun back to the car. 'Wait. Can you get me a coffee? I'll get some money from my bag.'

'Relax. It's all going on my work card. You don't have to pay.'

Half an hour later they sat at a picnic table with burgers, chips, juice and coffee. Dan lifted his takeaway mug to his lips. The smell was amazing.

'Careful. I asked the girl to make them extra hot so I could enjoy mine after I'd eaten.' Rodger gulped his juice. 'How long is it since you've been to the beach, Dan?'

'I've been trying to remember. It's like I've been here. I think maybe with Dad's parents before they went away. I would have been only a little kid. I remember that toilet block. Dad took me in there to belt me because I ran away.'

'Any other beaches?'

'I don't think so.'

'And haven't been back here since?'

Dan shook his head. He knew his school mates talked about the beach and going surfing on the weekends, but Dad never took him anywhere. He wriggled his toes in the sand and filled his mouth with fries. He'd never been interested in the beach before, but it brought a strange sense of calm, as though everything could be okay. 'Can I get here by train, Rodger?'

'Hmm. Maybe a bus. I'd have to check it. I guess I always drive.'

An emptiness fell on him. No car and no one to drive him anywhere. No mother. No school anymore. He pushed his half-eaten burger away and grabbed the coffee. It was hot, strong, creamy and wonderful. 'Wow. The coffee Dad drinks tastes nothing like this amazing concoction. Thanks, Rodger.'

'Your dad went north without you. He will be back soon. The police have a warrant out for his arrest.'

'His arrest? What for?' Dan wanted to run. Had they found Dad's drugs stash? But no. He'd have packed it. Maybe they'd found his tin. He stood. 'Thanks for the food. I need to go now.'

'Sit down, Dan. We need to talk. Your Dad's being charged for wilfully causing you bodily harm. Your collarbone has been broken in three places on three different occasions. You have concussion, deep tissue bruising and the list goes on. You won't be living with him any longer.'

 El Roi

Dan dropped himself to the seat, shaking, fear surging through every nerve ending. 'But... but... I never said it was Dad. I kept making silly mistakes and getting into fights and it's all my fault. If I was more careful and not so stupid. If I wasn't interested in books and maths but was strong like him and could throw bricks around...' His throat convulsed, trying to hold down the volcano rumbling deep in his belly. The pain exploded through his mouth in a wail. Horrified he clamped his hand on his mouth and fled. Down the beach, around drain pipes, through water he ran, trying to leave the savage pain behind. The beach stopped at the base of a rocky headland. He climbed the rock but waves crashed on his left and a chain wire fence stopped him on his right.

Exhausted, he collapsed onto a patch of sand between two rocks. There was only one arm to wrap across his belly. It was no match for the force pulsating through him.

'I hate him. I hate him. I hate him.' Sand flew as anger erupted through his feet.

The volcano ran its course. A hard core replaced the passion. Reality pushed him up and determined feet marched back the way he had come. 'I have no father. I have no need of a father. I will do this myself.'

Chapter 4

DAN'S NEW UNIT was in a different suburb. Someone had moved his belongings and made sure he had the basics, like a refrigerator. It wasn't fancy but he now lived alone. There'd been no word from Dad for weeks. He emptied the bean can and lobbed it at the bin. The missile hit its target. Dan grinned. Three in a row had hit dead centre. His head was recovering, helped by the fact no one had belted him for three months. Tomorrow he'd throw with his left hand. It was getting stronger and needed exercise. Tossing cans wasn't exactly what the physiotherapist had prescribed, but it was close enough. To celebrate, he drained his coke can and threw it towards the overflowing bin. It floated in a graceful arc, hit dead centre and rolled onto the floor. Dan air-punched with his left hand. With a sigh he picked an armload of cans off the floor and left for the bin. That was the problem living alone. No one to nag you to do stuff. He'd always done it, but only after someone had yelled at him.

Maybe fathers had some positive attributes. Nagging, bullying, buying food, paying rent... He dropped his load into the wheelie bin and wondered again what day he was supposed to take it out to the gutter. How was he to know if no one yelled at him?

In the kitchen he found a garbage bag in the corner. He tipped his clothes out of it, trying to find what he wanted. Would he need the bag for clothes again? But today's urgent need was rubbish.

Empty cans, chip packets, scrunched paper, food stuffs and the contents of the overflowing bin filled the bag. Tying it off, he dumped it in the wheelie bin and dragged it to the gutter. It stood alone. Not another bin lined the street. He air-punched again. *This week the best rubbish disposal award goes to Dan Furley, for winning the bin race.*

'It's not rubbish day today, boy.' The old lady yelled at him through a crack in her front window.

'Sorry. Just making sure I don't miss it.' Dan shoved his head down and took off.

'You stop right there, boy!'

He stopped. 'What?' It was rude, but no one was here to tell him what to do.

'Take that ugly, smelly thing back. I'm not looking at it for four more days.'

Dan strode back to the bin, twisted it around, and repositioned it behind the scraggly shrub on the footpath. Running, he passed her door, the weird guy's Buddha statue, the old man's flat, and kicked his own door open.

He glared back past the units and yelled, 'Don't tell me what to do. I am not "boy". I'm Dan and I'll do it my way.'

The door rattled on its hinges as it slammed behind him. Kicking clothes out of the way, he yanked the top drawer out

El Roi

of his desk. His fingers explored the cavity below the top, thankful it was still there. Lucky they brought the desk when they moved his stuff to this new place. *Ready Remedy*. As he prised the lid loose, there was a rap on the door.

'I'll do it my way.' The yell morphed to a squawk when the door opened and Rodger appeared.

'How's it working for you?'

'What?'

'Doing it your way. How's it working for you?'

The remedy tin was burning Dan's fingers. In panic he dropped it and kicked it under the bed. It was swallowed by a pile of dirty clothes. Rodger watched, leaning on the door frame. In four paces Dan was at the door. Rodger backed out, allowing him to slip out of the mess and shut the door. 'What are you doing here? I'm not one of your kids anymore.'

'No, you're an independent youth, but still a mate. I'm off work so I called in to see if you've eaten yet. We could get a burger or coffee?'

Dan kicked the step with his new sneaker. 'I'm broke, man.' How embarrassing. Rodger would know he shouldn't be broke. But when the money landed in his account it felt like a fortune. His new shoes were classy, but they didn't buy food.

'My shout.'

'Government card again.'

'No. I'd like to buy you a burger, Dan. What do you say?'

'I'll just change. I'll meet you in the car.' He slipped through the door and fell on his hands and knees, digging through the smelly clothes, his heart racing. Drugs and a filthy flat. How could he go out with Rodger after he'd seen the mess? At least he'd moved the rubbish.

His fingers closed around the tin. He returned it to its hidden chamber and shoved the drawer in place. His check shirt was on the clean side of the room. It was crumpled but it smelled okay.

'I've seen worse.' Rodger pulled the car from the curb and headed towards the lights.

Dan focussed on the front yards of his new neighbours. He didn't need to. He'd walked this way to school for six weeks now, but what could he say? What did Rodger mean?

'And I've smelt worse.' The car accelerated away from the lights. 'I don't let everyone in my car, you know. If they smell, I suggest a walk. It's good exercise.'

'How many kids do you follow up on?'

'I'll call and see most of them and offer friendship. Most swear at me and slam the door in my face or worse. I don't try again. Not because I don't care, but I have to respect their right to choose their own company. But you're different from most, Dan.' He lapsed into silence. They passed several burger joints and turned toward the city. The next four sets of lights were all green. Rodger switched to the right lane and they dropped into a tunnel.

'I've never driven in a tunnel. It's cool.'

'It gets me places sooner. I think we will use two tonight.'

Dan read signs and watched exits. At first the names were familiar—AIRPORT, CITY, GOLD COAST—but then they meant little to him. Rodger took an exit marked *Toowong*. Dan's stomach turned. He'd have no way of getting home if Rodger dumped him.

'It's okay. I intend to take you home.'

'You reading my mind?'

          El Roi

Rodger laughed. 'Didn't mean to. Just realised I've taken you out of your comfort zone after offering you a burger. I had this sudden idea. Have you ever been to Mt Coot-tha?'

'Dunno. But I doubt it.' The car dropped a gear as the road steepened in front of them.

Dan stared out the window, amazed. 'Look at those lights. You can see a lot from this road.'

His companion laughed again. 'Mountains are like that!'

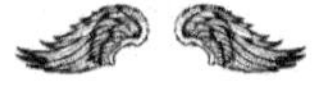

'DID YOU LEAVE A LIGHT on in the flat, Dan?' Rodger balled the empty burger bag and tossed it from one hand to the other.

'No. It was daylight.'

Rodger gazed out over the sea of city lights from the viewing platform. 'That explains it then.'

'Explains what?'

Rodger waved the crumpled bag across the city view. 'Why I can't pick your place out.'

Dan threw his squashed bag at Rodger, hitting his ear. 'And which light is your place?'

'Can't see my place. It's further to the north.'

Down below them a zillion gemstones glittered, mesmerising Dan. Streetlights that were orange-gold, diamond-white. Headlights on a plane winked at him, strings of red rubies shimmered as cars moved along freeways. Stars hung just out of reach above him. 'When I get a car, I'm going to bring Amalya here.'

'Who is Amalya?'

'Just a girl.' He walked to the rail. He hadn't seen her since the day he told her he wanted to marry her. He hadn't caught the same train since that morning. He had no number. And still no phone. 'Do you think there is any way I could get a phone, Rodger?'

'You just need money, but not much to get a simple one.'

'Should've got a phone instead of these runners. I just saw these and liked them.'

'It's a good goal. And everyone needs something to aim for.'

Dan turned and looked at him in the gloom. 'I can hit targets. My aim is straight.'

'Good. You will need skill and determination to reach your goal.'

'Yeah. How to get the girl.'

'How to get the car.'

'I don't even throw when I don't think I can hit the target.' As the words came out of his mouth, Dan saw his bin with cans lying all around it. 'Not always true...'

Rodger waved to the view. 'Can you see the city centre?'

'Where the tall buildings are?'

'Yes. Ever been there?'

Lights were intense amongst those skyscrapers. Some lit every floor. 'What's the white circle?'

'It's called the Eye of Brisbane—a Ferris wheel. We could go and look.'

A spark burned in Dan's belly. 'Let's go.'

'Wait.' Rodger turned back to the lights. 'We need a plan. How do we get there?'

The spark snuffed out. 'Don't you know?'

'You can see the city. Can you see any route leading there?'

El Roi

Dan looked at the lights, wondering what to say to this crazy guy. All that lay before him were masses of gathered lights. But there were roads. They all went in the wrong direction. Only one road he could see went in the right direction, but it seemed to have no beginning and melted into oblivion before it reached the city centre. He shrugged and pointed. 'That road?'

Rodger agreed. 'Milton Road. We can use it. But how can we get to it?'

'I don't have any idea. I don't even know how to get home. Why are you asking me all these questions?' Frustration boiled in Dan. 'I have enough impossibilities in my life without you adding more.'

'Come. I'll show you.'

The Commodore glided down the mountain. Rodger steered it around a roundabout and on to a main road. 'To reach any goal you just have to take lots of little steps. First step, get off the mountain. Second step: when choices come, like the roundabout, select the correct direction. There are always other roads leading us away from our destination.'

'You're sounding like a school teacher.' Dan slipped down in his seat and closed his eyes. He wanted to be home, be alone. He needed think time, not some lecture from a guy who had an education, a family, a job, a car and probably a girl.

'Do you have a girlfriend, Rodger?'

'A beautiful wife.'

'You're married! Do you hit her often?' How did the question escape his mouth? He gulped, hoping to take the words back, to swallow his horror. As the drumming in his ears lessened, the only noise was the motor and the tyres on the road. Maybe Rodge the Dodge didn't hear.

The car stopped. Dan could see the red light, but nothing else. He was too low in his seat.

As the car pulled away from the lights Rodger spoke. 'My Lizzie is so precious to me, I'd do anything to guard and protect her—make sure she never gets hurt.'

'Does she cook well?' Why was he asking such idiot questions? What did it matter?

'We are both learning to cook. We've had a few disasters. We put meat on to cook one morning. The book said to cook for six hours on low. Just as I was shutting the front door I smelt something funny. The meat was burning. Smoke filled the kitchen. I grabbed the pan, and shoved it under the tap. It made a shocking mess.

'Was Lizzie angry?'

'No. We found out later the recipe we were following was for a Slow Cooker. We laugh a lot about that incident.'

Rodger slowed for another red light. 'Home to the left. City to the right. What would you prefer, Dan?'

'Home... I mean... do you mind if we go home? Will Lizzie be upset you spent so much time with me?'

'She's at college tonight, but she encourages me.'

'To do what?'

'I often call and see one of my boys on Thursday nights. Friday nights we lead a youth group together. Would you like to come?'

'What's a youth group?'

'Just a group of kids your age and older. We play games, hang out, sing a bit and talk about God.'

El Roi

Dan sat up straight. 'God? What God?'

'The God of gods. The Creator of the Universe? My heavenly Father.'

'God is a Father?'

'Yes. He had one Son, Jesus. And now He has many sons. I am one of them. You can be too if you want.'

'I don't want any rotten father anywhere near me, even if He does call Himself God.' A fire raged in the pit of his belly, sending flashes of heat and anger through his chest and down his arms. Cold hard fear blended with it, churning his gut over and over. He shoved his fist into his mouth, to plug it, to stop words escaping or the half-digested burger from decorating the glove box of the Commodore.

The car slowed at a set of lights Dan recognised. As soon as it stopped he swung the door open, jumped out and ran down the dark side street.

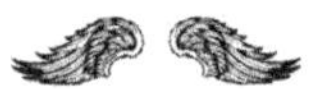

AT HOME, DAN CLICKED the door behind him and pulled the brown curtains, making sure there were no cracks. He didn't need a father, his or God or anyone. He could look after himself without any no-good, interfering superior telling him what to do.

Yeah. I can see that. A wheedling voice in his head mocked him. Yeah. You've got clean clothes, lots of money and plenty of food. Let's count your cash, Dan. Grab your phone and check the bank like the big shot kids at school.

Angry, Dan pulled out the drawer again. With the tin open and pages sliced out of the little red Bible, he portioned out the hash. There was enough for four smokes, maybe five if he stretched it. Four rolled up well, edges sealed, ends trimmed with the blade from his Bible. The fifth one looked a little lean. He'd offer it to a newbie at a special price. Satisfied, he cleaned everything away and tidied up.

See. He addressed the wheedling voice in his head. *Everything is clean, tomorrow I'll have cash and soon I'll have a cash card and a phone. So there.*

The voice didn't respond. Dan found a clear spot on his bed and curled in a ball. As he started to doze a roundabout loomed in his head. He took the exit declaring Wrong Way— Go Back.

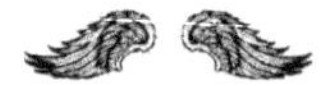

It was the last day of term. Dan leaned on the administration counter at school. No one was coming. He couldn't see anyone anywhere. Maybe he could retrieve the smokes from above the door. Two more sales would be mighty helpful. He edged up the hall, every nerve at attention. Just a few more steps to go. There was no one at the desk, no one in the hall. His heart pumped in his throat.

He lifted his hand. The door swished open. His whole body leapt to the left.

'Dan!' Mrs Rhodes grinned at him. 'Did you hear me calling you? I was just saying to Mr Blueberry I hoped to see you before the term closed.'

Floral perfume surrounded him. His nerves collapsed like sails becalmed. 'Mrs Rose... I mean Rhodes... I'm sorry Mrs Rose Rhodes.'

Her laugh swept through him like wind in a garden, picking up his shattered nerves. 'Have you got a few minutes?'

    El Roi

'I... I was just going to ask for my report card.'

'They're not finished, but on the whole you've done quite well. That's why I wanted to talk to you. They will post it after school closes for the year.'

'I hope they don't send it to my father.'

A horrified look flashed across her face, and she marched to the desk, calling out instructions to the young woman who appeared from the back room. Mrs Rhodes led him down the hall to another office. She waved to her name on the door as she clicked her door open. 'Look! My own room, just as the year ends! Come in. Take a seat. Soft drink? I'm having coffee.'

'Can I have a coffee? There's none at my place. I haven't had one for three weeks, not since Rodger...' The wonderful coffee aroma blended with her perfume. He slumped into one of her couches and sighed. 'This feels like home.'

'Your flat doesn't?'

'No people, not much furniture. Smells bad. No coffee... and... and did I say no one?'

She passed him a cup. The first sip scalded his tongue, but it was hot, sweet and milky. 'Thank you. It's wonderful.'

'Lonely, Dan?' Grey eyes with a hint of blue caressed him. He looked at his shoes and sipped more coffee. He was used to eyes glaring or accusing or being angry, but these eyes were soft, caring and gentle.

'I'm doing fine.'

'What are you doing in the holidays?'

'I got stuff to do.'

'Interested in a job?'

'I tried Maccas, but it'd drive me crazy. Same thing over and over. Everyone yelling at me. I'd probably explode and...'

'I wasn't thinking of Maccas. I know a guy who needs help in a computer shop.'

'I don't know much about computers. I use the ones at school, but we've never owned one.'

Her grey eyes turned bluish as they opened wide. 'But your assignments? How...'

'School library... and the council library let me work on theirs. Some I hand write.'

'That answers the next question.'

Dan swallowed the rest of his coffee and looked hopefully at the jar. 'What question?'

'I had selected a couple of holiday courses for you to do to help lift your English mark. But if you don't have a computer...'

'Or internet access, except the library. Could I do them there?'

'You're interested?'

'And bored.'

She chuckled. 'I thought a job would be good.'

'Who is it? I could go and talk to them. If it's selling, I reckon I could do that.'

Mrs Rhodes handed him a business card and waved to a machine in the corner of the room. 'Run yourself a copy.'

Back at his seat, his mug steamed, refilled with coffee. A plate of chocolate biscuits beckoned him. He was so hungry he could've swallowed two biscuits whole. Instead he offered her the plate. 'Would you like one?'

She laughed. 'Biscuits fill young men's hollow legs. If I had one, you'd see it on my waist tomorrow.'

'I sure got hollow legs.' Six biscuits slid into his stomach before he realised he was eating like a pig. Heat flooded his

El Roi

face. His Mum would clip his ears and send him to bed. He stood. 'I'm sorry for my bad manners, Miss. I'll go now.'

She stood to her full stature but had to tilt her head to look into his eyes. 'Sit, Dan. You haven't drunk your coffee.' Four more biscuits landed on the plate. 'And finish them up. They'll go stale during the holidays.'

Sitting, he sipped the coffee, trying to steady his hand. It was just as his dad always said. He always stuffed up. He needed to get out of this office.

'Have you ever slammed a Tim Tam?' Grey eyes danced from the other side of the desk. 'You haven't, I can tell. One of life's great skills. It's easy. Bite a little of both ends of the biscuit.'

Was she testing him? *Having a go at me?* Her sparkling eyes urged him on. 'Go on. Just do it. Then you dip it in your coffee and use the biscuit like a straw.'

With one end in his coffee and one end in his mouth, he sucked. Nothing happened.

'C'mon. Strong pull.'

Smooth chocolate swirling in hot coffee slid down his throat. *Heaven.* He pulled coffee through it again.

'Now swallow the biscuit before it collapses.'

While he was still trying to decipher what she meant, the biscuit disintegrated in his hand and fell into his coffee.

Roaring laughter filled the room. 'Your eyes, your face! Oh my. You did enjoy that!'

Another cup of coffee landed in front of him. 'Want to try again?'

When he left the room he had details of a job, log in details for an online course and a one hundred dollar voucher for Woolworths. A hand-written shopping list, compiled by a tiny teacher who smelled like flowers, lay in his pocket beside an unsold rollie.

El Roi

Chapter 5

Students poured out the gate, bubbling with chatter and excitement. Summer holidays were here. Around him flowed conversations about holidays and families. Some of the group had their own cars and were making plans. He hung back. These conversations unsettled him and stirred anger in his belly. He didn't have any family or a car and there was no hope of it ever happening. He booted a stray pebble into a rubbish bin and stormed down the street.

'Hey, Dan.' One of the nerdy kids from his English class puffed up behind him.

'What?' He glared at him over one shoulder. Was he Edgar or Ian? He couldn't remember.

'Hey, Dan.' The guy groaned as he moved a heavy pack from one shoulder to the other. 'Should've taken stuff home days ago. You got much in your bag?'

'No. I took most of mine yesterday.' The truth was he didn't have much, but he wasn't telling this guy who carried a laptop and an iPad to every class. 'How can I help ya?'

'Just have a message for you.' He juggled his pack again. Dan fingered the rollie in his pocket. Maybe this would lead to a sale.

'The girl on the train. You know the one you always sat with?'

Dan's heart skipped a beat. 'Yeah.'

'She was asking after you. Wanting to know why you disappeared.'

'What did you say, man?'

'I told her you never caught this train anymore.'

'What did she say?' His nerves tapped the side of his neck.

'Not much, but she said to say hello.'

Without thinking, Dan followed Edgar or Ian down the ramp to the station.

'I thought you didn't get the train anymore.'

'I don't... but would she be on this one?' As he spoke metal wheels screeched as a train rounded the corner.

'Her school is on the next train.' His messenger waved and jumped into a carriage.

Retreating out of the heat, Dan leaned against the station master's office. Would he dare? Really, he owed Amalya an explanation. Why hadn't he thought of catching a train before? He could easily return. No one would miss him. What did it matter if he was late?

He chose the second front carriage. Her school's uniforms were scattered throughout the carriage. Scanning every face he walked the length of the rail car. She wasn't there. The next carriage was jammed full with screaming year eights. She'd never stay in this cage with them. By the time he neared his old station he'd searched the length of the train twice. Not there. Part of him slumped with disappointment, the other

El Roi

part sighed with relief. Who was he to think she'd even care for him anyway?

'Dan?' A short kid with glasses perched on an upturned nose touched his arm. A couple of giggling girls supported her.

'Yes. Do I know you?'

'I live in Milly's street. Year Tens finished yesterday.'

'Milly?'

'I call her that. Sometimes she calls herself Amalya.'

'You know Amalya? Can you give her a message from me?'

'Yeah, but they left on holidays yesterday. I'll tell her I saw you when she gets back.'

'Can you tell her I was looking for her?'

The girls giggled. 'Sure can.'

The train's brakes hissed and it lurched to a stop. He escaped the girls and jumped onto the familiar platform. A bored-looking guy was checking tickets at the exit so he jumped the fence and followed his old path. It felt strange to be back. The old fear turned his gut as it had every day when he wondered what waited for him at home. A track led him across an overgrown park. He averted his eyes from the kids' playground where he'd rocked his pain for hours, swinging in the dark.

Half a block from his old house, he stopped. What would even make him revisit these places of torment? Spinning on his heel, he started to retrace his steps. A familiar shape turned the corner and walked toward him.

'Dan! Dan Furley! Well, I be blowed. Is Alf back, too?' One of Dad's old drinking cronies grinned as though he'd won the lottery.

'I'm just taking a walk while I wait for a train. Gotta get back or I'll miss it.'

'I'll walk with you. Anything to avoid the Missus. She's in a savage mood today.' He puffed as he tried to keep up with Dan. 'Hey, Dan. Got time for a couple of quickies at the pub with an old family friend?'

'You know I'm too young. Pub won't serve me anything but lemonade. Besides, I'm broke.'

'Silly laws. Look at you. Big enough to be a man.'

Only a block and he could escape to the station. Dan lengthened his stride, but fingers grabbed his elbow. 'Ever had a joint, Dan? I've got a couple. Want to join me?'

'Don't touch...' Dan slowed his pace. He was out of product. Selling rollies made better money than a computer shop could offer for less time. '...don't smoke them myself, but I'll join you.'

'You should try one. All your problems, money, nagging women, boss's garbage. They all disappear. It's Friday night. A bloke deserves a break.'

Voices warred in Dan's head. One egged him on; the other told him to go home. But what was home? An empty bedsit with little food, messy clothes and no mother. *Face it, Dan. There is no home to go to and no one to miss you.* He followed his host down a walkway between houses and through a slatted gate.

Three soft raps on the metal door and it squeaked open a crack. 'It's Edgar the beggar! Did the dragon let you out of jail?'

Dan was yanked in behind Edgar, and the door clanged shut. Why did it sound like a prison door? He blinked, trying

El Roi

to focus in the sudden gloom. The odour was overwhelming. Engine oil, grease, dust and the distinctive smell of marijuana smoke assaulted him. The metal clad space was filled with junk, but in the centre about five men sat on drums, an old rider mower and other odd shaped bits of metal.

'Who is this, Edgar?' The voice had a metallic sound, setting Dan's teeth on edge.

All banter stopped. Every bloodshot eye glared at Dan. He backed toward the door but the escape was blocked by a wiry, red-haired midget. His hands were on his hips, balled. His eyes darted as if the devil was after him. *Mick!* Dan swallowed the bile that rushed to his mouth. Visions raced through his brain. Mick drunk with his dad, swaying like a madman, demanding Dan dance naked on the kitchen table.

'Long time no see, Mick.' Dan stuck out his hand, and made himself look in the haunted eyes and wait. And wait. And wait. He knew the drill. He who speaks first loses.

'I never seen you before in my life.' Mick lifted his fist from his hips.

Edgar laughed, slapping his thigh. 'You don't recognise him. You've known him for years. Sit down, Mick, and have another smoke.'

'You haven't answered my question, Edgar. You know the rules. Only family.' Dan didn't recognise the face with the metal tongue. He decided he'd stay near the door.

'He is family, Sol. This...' He pulled Dan forward and slapped his back. 'This is Alf's son, Dan.' He grinned as though he presented a prize bull. 'Grab a chair, Dan. Someone pass me a smoke or a drink. A man could die waiting with you morons on the warpath.'

A match flared, Sol drew hard and passed the weed on before blowing a great cloud of smoke in Dan's face. 'Sit, kid.'

'I'm fine, thanks.'

Sol pulled out a stump of wood. 'I said... *sit*.'

The stump was low. It put him at a disadvantage, but there was no other option. He sat. At least he'd be faster than anyone in the room. Mick leaned against the fender of the ride-on and pulled on the smoke, passing it to Dan. To smoke or not. He'd never been so close, never had a live one in his fingers. He lifted it to his mouth but passed it on to Edgar.

'You didn't smoke!' Sol jumped to his feet, eyes darting, nerves flicking in his neck. 'Why are you here if you're not smoking?'

Mick was on his feet and another bearish man lumbered to his feet. Only one guy seemed unmoved. A smaller guy leaned back in the shadows where Dan couldn't grasp any defining features. Dan's chest vibrated as adrenaline kicked in. The door was blocked, the drug-crazed men circled like dogs.

Sol re-offered the rolled weed, his hand digging in his pocket. He pulled out two white pills. 'Take your choice, kid. Smoke with us or these little beauties will find their way down your throat.'

Nervous eyes monitored his every breath, glaring, waiting, gloating. Outnumbered, he reached out to take the smoke, but something rose up in him. He too would look like them if he wasn't careful. 'Sorry, men.' He smiled at them. 'Edgar knew I wasn't going to smoke. I never do when working.'

'Working?'

'Yup. Got to be on the ball when doing deals.'

El Roi

'Deals? What do you mean?' Sol passed the weed without taking a smoke. 'I'd be interested in hearing about these deals.'

'I was looking for Fred. Dad called him Red Fred.'

Sol glanced across the room at the shadowed figure perched on a filthy drum. 'What would you be wanting with Fred?'

'My business, I reckon. But if you can't help me...' Dan dared to look at each one. All the eyes slipped sideways, except one. The guy on the drum leaned forward and lifted black eyes. Dan felt them probe at his depths before they dropped back to the ground.

Dan pulled himself off the stump and held his hand to Sol. 'Thanks for having me.'

Sol ignored the offered hand and waved Dan back to the stump. Mick lumbered to lean on the door. 'Not so fast, kid.'

'He's okay, men. No need to panic. He's Alf's son.' The voice didn't match the black eyes. It was soft, refined, nearly but not quite oily. He nodded at Mick who opened the door.

Dan made his legs walk the stride of the free, but everything in him wanted to run. In the walkway he lengthened his stride.

'Wait.' The voice carried authority, and he felt like he was back in Blueberry's office. 'I'm Fred. You wanted me?' The refined voice belonged to the black eyes. Dan faltered, heart flipped over. He stopped. 'How can I help you, kid?'

He turned, scrambling to find words. 'You seen my dad?' Any conversation was better than the one he wanted to start.

'Nah! He left town in a hurry. Coppers waiting for him so don't think we'll be seeing him for a while.'

'What the coppers want him for?' He held his breath. Maybe they discovered he murdered Mum. Maybe he was sprung with dope, or the tax guys caught him. Dad always worried about the tax guys.

'Story goes they want to charge him for grievous bodily harm inflicted on a minor.' The guy stood shoulder to shoulder with Dan. Together they left the walkway and headed down the street. 'I don't think he'll be back in a hurry. Do you need him for something?'

A familiar heat exploded in Dan's belly, and he booted a discarded Maccas bag into a fence. 'Nothing. Just checking he wasn't waiting for me round the next corner.'

'Must be tough without a dad?'

Dan eyed Fred. He was behaving like Mrs Rhodes or Rodger. He'd need to be careful. It felt like a trap. He squared his shoulders and walked faster. 'I can look after myself. Who needs a dad anyway? Life's easier without one.'

'Burger?' Fred waved toward a dirty-looking, old-fashioned burger joint.

'In there?'

'Best burgers for miles around but don't tell anyone. Makes the queue too long.' Fred disappeared through coloured plastic strips.

A burger? He'd love a burger. The chocolate biscuits had left a gaping hole in his gut. Dan shoved his hands in his pockets. Only a rollie and he didn't think they'd accept it as payment. Then there'd be nothing to sell. If he grabbed the next train, he'd be able to forget this crazy adventure and relax. If there wasn't a guard checking passes. But he needed more supply.

Crossing the street, he slouched on a bench under a tree, out of the glaring street light. If he was a kid, he'd make a decision using eeny, meeny, miney, mo. Would he ask Fred

El Roi

about supply, or would he run while he had the chance? A coin! If he had one, he could toss it. Heads for leave. No. Tails for being a coward and running away with his tail between his legs. He was still digging in his backpack looking for a coin when Fred pushed through the door. He glanced around, before crossing the street.

'Catch.' A can of Coke whistled through the air. Dan pulled it in with his left hand.

'Good catch.'

'Rotten throw.'

'Smart-mouthed kid.'

'Headmaster voice.'

'Watch your mouth, Furley.'

Dan's heart leapt to his mouth. His brain spun. This dude had nothing on him. There was no reason for fear... not until he'd became a client. Humour was the only way forward. He formed his duckbill face and stared down through crossed eyes.

'What do you think you're doing?' Fred's eyes questioned him.

Dan stretched his mouth back to shape. 'Watching my mouth, as you said, Sir.'

Fred's laughter made the teens on the other side of the road turn and stare. 'No wonder Alf lost his cool with you occasionally. You've got a quick mouth.'

'And a quick brain. Dad hated my brain because it was faster than his.'

'You and I should talk. I think we'd work well together.' Fred jumped as his pocket beeped. 'Burgers are waiting. Let's go find a good place to talk.'

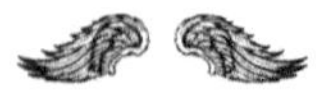

Dan scaled the paling fence and dropped into the backyard of his block of units. He pumped the air. Yes, he was right behind the bush. Last couple of times he'd tried this at night, the sensor light had caught him. Tonight he crept behind the bushes on the back side of the four commission units and emerged onto the front street. Let the old biddies' lights turn on now. He was coming into his own house through his own front door and if anyone had followed they wouldn't know where he'd disappeared to.

Ready Remedy received its new stock without complaint. Tomorrow he'd craft six of his minis. He had a promise of another free burger at eight o'clock on Sunday night and a bill to pay. There were plenty of parties happening on the weekend. Five sales would meet the debt. Six would be better, seven and he'd start to pile up cash for a phone. A working man needed a contact.

Feeling dirty, he decided to shower. His dirty clothes were balled and belted into the dirty corner near the bathroom door. Hot water flooded the long blond hair hanging over his eyes. *Are you blinded or blinkered, Dan?* Flicking the hair off his face he ignored the question and lathered his hands till bubbles squeezed between his fingers. But somehow his hands still felt dirty, as though they'd been in the sewer.

Damp and naked he lay on crumpled sheets and tried to ignore the stale sweaty smell. Just before he fell asleep a pair of soft grey eyes danced at the edge of his vision. He groaned. At least he wouldn't see her for seven whole weeks. He'd quit his job then and become the perfect student, with a laptop.

 El Roi

Chapter 6

The Second Sunday evening Dan sat on the park bench opposite the burger joint, shading his eyes from the setting sun. Tonight he'd buy his own burger. Might even buy Fred's. And he would pay cash for his stock. His business was booming. Selling dirty minis, as he called his product, wasn't making him rich, but life was easier. Maybe this week he'd be able to buy a phone.

A battered grey Land Rover parked up the street. He wanted a decent car, or even a twin cab ute. A blue one. A group of long-legged girls emerged from the shop and laughed as they headed toward a pink VW. He pulled a long face. Who in their right mind would drive a pink car?

'Enjoying the scenery?' Fred dropped on the seat beside him.

'Just thinking how ugly that pink car is.' He turned and shook Fred's hand.

'At your age you should be ogling the birds with the long legs.'

'Birds? Sorry, mate. Thinking about cars. Can I buy you a burger?'

Fred slapped him on the shoulder and grinned. 'The Missus has invited you for dinner.'

'Dinner?'

'Yeah. You remember. Home-cooked food on plates at a table. You have had dinner before?'

'Um. Sometimes.' Dan's throat closed over. He couldn't go to someone's house. What if he stuffed up?

'Come on. Mustn't keep the lady waiting.' Fred stood and walked toward the beaten-up Land Rover.

'Wait. I can't... I mean... thanks but...'

The door squeaked on a rusty hinge and Fred waved him in. 'Get in. We have business to attend to and a man must eat. Besides, Ginny is the best cook in town.' Fred spun the wheel and returned from the direction he had come. 'You got much stock left?'

'None. And enough dough to do a cash deal.'

'You're cool enough to sell an order of hash and you're terrified of having dinner at my place?'

'I know the street. I don't know much about...'

'Family?'

Dan slumped in the seat. *Family.* He had had one... of sorts.

'Family frightens you, Dan?'

'It's unsafe... the rules change... don't know what I'm supposed to do.'

'They're not all like that, Dan.' He spun the Rover into a yard and parked beside the drive under a tree. 'We have four kids. Bazza, Callie, Florida and Sebastian.'

Dan wiped his clammy hands on the sides of his new surf shorts and followed. Fred waited at the door and ushered him in.

El Roi

The meal table was wild. The table was covered with random dishes of different colours and foods he couldn't identify. But the smell had his tastebuds watering. Ginny waved him to a seat. 'Help yourself, Dan.' Her smile went deep into her blue eyes. *Soft.* Another soft lady.

Dan looked at the table. His stomach turned. He didn't know what to take, how to do it. Fred grabbed a flat disk and laid it on his plate. 'Grab one, Dan. I make the best burritos ever. Just follow me.'

'Don't do what Dad does unless you want your mouth burned out.' Bazza threw a disk on his plate and covered it with mince out of a bowl. 'Give it here and I'll do the meat for you. Pass the sour cream, Callie. Florrie, stop stealing all the cheese.'

Dan watched as bowls flew around the table, sauce splashed and food was rolled. It was fun and terrifying. There were too many decisions, too much room for error. A gentle hand on his shoulder made him turn. 'Take this one, Dan. I made it for you.' Ginny patted his shoulder and took the plate from in front of him. 'Taste and tell me if it's okay or not. If you don't like it, we can try again.'

She took the spare chair beside Fred and slathered cream on the mince.

Dan took a bite. Flavours caressed his tastebuds. It was better, much better than a burger. Kids laughed, cried and argued around him. Everyone talked at once. Multiple conversations raged like a school yard around a table.

'Dan.' Ginny called him through the chaos. 'Do you have brothers or sisters?'

'Uh... um. Yes, I guess so. Two little sisters. I haven't seen them since Mum...'

'Where's your mother, Dan?'

'She disappeared. I... I wonder if she's dead.' Dan dropped the last bit of his third burrito, shaking away tears pushing past his defences. Every eye on the table looked at him.

'Did she eat too much?' Sebastian's eyes were wide and blue like his mothers. 'My fish died when it ate too much. We flushed...'

'Sebastian! That's enough. Callie, pass me some more chilli sauce.'

The noise resumed. Dan picked up his dinner and finished it.

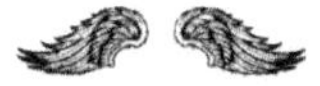

THE DOORS SLAMMED and the Land Rover lumbered down the road. Dan's body tingled from Ginny's hug. Somehow the chaos melted into bedrooms and all was quiet when they'd left the house. His head still spun from the noise but his heart was warm.

'Sorry, Dan. I forget how loud they are. I guess we are used to four kids.'

'It was fun, a lot of fun and great food. Thanks, Fred.'

'Where to?'

'Um... the station?'

'I'll drive you home. Not dropping you at the station alone at this hour of night.'

'Fred. You are weird.'

El Roi

His laugh was always loud. That was another strange thing. He spoke softly, gently, yet no one disobeyed him. His laugh was loud.

'In what way?'

'You're a dealer, yet you drive an old Land Rover. You can stand up to anyone in Sol's shed yet you're a family man. You remind me of a headmaster, but you're selling me hash.'

'I wish I wasn't selling you hash. It's not good for me and it's not good for you.'

'Then why?'

'Long story, but I got caught and owed this guy a lot of money. He threatened to bankrupt me, take my house. The alternative was to become one of his traders and pay off the debt.'

'Does Ginny know?'

The van stopped between Maccas and a chemist. The spot was very public, yet shaded from street lighting. 'My poor Ginny would have a fit. She must never know.'

'Have you paid the guy yet?'

'No... and I'm starting to think he has me trapped. He keeps changing the rules.' Fred reached up under the seat. 'Same amount as last week, or double?'

'Same will be enough. I'm thinking I'll try and get another job as well.' He pulled a wad of notes out of his backpack.

Fred took it without counting it. 'Now, where to?'

Dan gave him his address. He hadn't planned to trust him, but he found he did. He was scared for Fred. If the coppers caught Dan, he had nothing to lose. But that whole family relied on Fred.

'Get a job, Dan. Build a future for yourself. No one else will.' He pulled up in front of the units. The Rover stopped with a cough and Dan opened the door.

'Thanks. I had a great night.'

'Dan.'

'Yeah.' Something made him pause and wait.

'Dan, I never heard your mother died. Did Alf tell you that?'

'No... but he beat her so bad and... she... she... disappeared.'

'The pig.' Fred jumped out of the car and came to Dan on the footpath. 'I'm sorry, son. No one should have to suffer like that.'

'Thanks.' Dan fled. He could handle violence, but kindness broke something inside him.

He slammed the door shut behind him and threw himself on the bed. It was as lumpy as his heart rate. Standing up, he cleared the bed, throwing clothes, folders and one of his old shoes in all directions. The boot hit the opposite wall and slid to the floor.

An answering thump on the wall silenced him for a little. He found a pillow, buried his head and wailed. *If you're alive, Mum, why didn't you come back for me?* His father's sneering voice answered. *She always loved the girls more than us. We men have to stick together.*

He smashed the pillow into the floor and drank water straight from the tap. In the dark, he sank onto the floor and sobbed. It didn't matter. No one could see him. No one cared. His head throbbed, but the pain in his heart doubled him over. Maybe he'd die. He'd rather take a belting than deal with this pain. He could try frozen peas on his chest... but there was nothing frozen.

 El Roi

Curled in a ball, his head kept replaying images from his night with Fred. Sebastian curled up on his mother's lap until he slept. Fred kissing his forehead as he bent to carry him to bed. Ginny pulling Callie into a hug after she cleared the table. 'Thanks, beautiful girl.' Wrestling with Bazza on the floor without getting into trouble. Fred separating the kids when they fought but not adding to the belting.

His pain intensified. Panadol. He needed pain relief. He needed drugs. *Drugs... of course... I have drugs.*

He slashed a full page from the Bible. '*God sets the lonely in families.*' The words jumped off the page. He wiped his blurry eyes and checked. *Rubbish, God. Rubbish. You took my family and left me lonely.*

He tipped a pile of hash on the words and rolled a smoke. A fat one, a clean one, a big one. After he licked the side on the paper, he ran his finger the full length to seal it. Both ends were screwed tight. He didn't want to lose a drop. He checked his craftsmanship, as always. Satisfied, he put it in his mouth. *You gunna really send six or seven minis up in smoke? What's happened to your brain?*

He rolled the smoke away across the floor and rocked back and forth, head between his knees. The pain will pass. How can it? No family, no hope. The argument raged in his mind, tormenting him, torturing him. He sprung to his feet, snatched up the smoke and searched for matches, a lighter, anything. But there was nothing. The old guy who just banged on the wall—he'd have a light. It was his ashtray that supplied Dan with tobacco to mix with the hash and make his dirty minis.

Smoke between his fingers, he marched next door and knocked.

'Who's there?'

'I just need a light, if you don't mind.' His voice shook but his manners were intact, he noted with disgust.

The door opened a crack and the old guy peered out. 'Oh. It's you.' The door shut and Dan heard him pull back the security chain. 'Come on in. I'm Jack. Can't be too careful these days. Never know when some drug-starved moron will attack.'

With a quick flick, a flame waited. Dan grasped his smoke between his lips and leaned to the flame. The flame died. The smoke was snatched out of his mouth and thrown on top of the overflowing ashtray.

'A rollie... with no filter! Can't let you pollute yourself with such rubbish.' The old guy flicked open a packet of smokes and pulled out two. 'Here. Have a decent smoke. These menthols are the best money can buy. Just as well I get them cheap.' He lit one and passed it to Dan, lighting another for himself.

With the cigarette hanging from his mouth he grabbed two beers out of the fridge. He tossed one to Dan who nearly dropped the cigarette trying to catch it.

'Sit, boy. You look as though you need a stiff drink.' He waved towards a worn over-stuffed lounge, then sank into the single recliner. His ashtray was on his right, with the TV remote. Newspapers, beer cans and his glasses balanced on a small table to his left. Dan's smoke balanced on the spent butts, getting sprayed with ash as Jack tapped his smoke after every draw.

El Roi

Dan's chest pain was replaced by raw fear. How could he be so careless? Evidence of his drug dealing seemed to glow in front of him.

'Are you going to smoke or not?'

Dan lifted the smoke to his mouth. He knew how to do it. He'd watched his father for years and sworn never to touch tobacco. Smoke in the corner of your mouth, big draw, blow smoke. He drew long… then doubled over coughing and gasping.

Jack lumbered over and slapped him on the back. 'You've never smoked, have you? You don't try to draw deep with your L plates.'

Tears rolled down Dan's face as his lungs seemed to explode, rejecting the invader. He struggled out of the chair and butted the cigarette out in the ash tray. With his back to Jack, he retrieved his rollie and bolted for the door. 'S… sorry.' He was still coughing when he leaned against his closed door.

Sore throat, aching lungs, a sword piercing his heart. He curled into a ball on his bed, his pillow a poor substitute for the teddy he longed for. Was the lid of the beans tin sharp enough to slash his wrists? He should've grabbed the beer bottle. There must be something he could break and then he'd cut his throat. His brain told his body to get up. But it was too hard… all too hard.

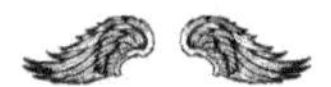

Family! Family! You belong to us. You've been put in our family. Creatures were closing in on him. Dan ran, his heart racing. Adrenaline pumped his feet faster. He needed somewhere to hide. A quick glance over his shoulder showed about six of

them, loping on all four legs, dark hair, black—or was it dark brown?—flowing from distorted heads.

The largest one caught his eye. Come to daddy. I'm your daddy. You've made your choice. Now you're mine.

The trees were closing in, but up ahead was a light, a faint glimmer. He pushed his legs harder. If he could just get to the light... to the light... He caught a vine and swung, getting closer, closer. But one of them loomed in front of him. You're ours now. Our family. Our family. *The light, he must get to the light. Another monster popped up.* No way to get there. Too late. You're family.

Another on his left, six closing behind him... Long hairy black arms reached out...

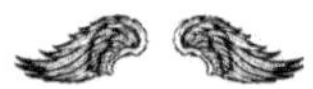

Screaming, sweating, panting, pulse racing, he forced open one eye. No trees. No hands. No cackling voices. He clung to his bed head, threading one arm through the rough timber slats, the other hand clinging to his damp pillow. Every time he closed his eyes, they gloated from a distance. *Light.* He needed light.

He released the bed and jumped across the room, flicking the switch. Bright. It was too bright. He turned it off, but the darkness was darker than before. Covering his eyes, he flicked the switch again and crept to his bed, hiding his head under the pillow, heart racing. 'Mummy. Mummy, I'm scared.' He knew she wouldn't come, but it brought some comfort and he fell into a troubled doze.

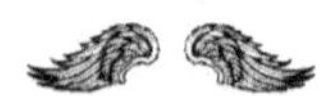

 El Roi

I'm your new Mummy. Come, let me hold you. Come close, come... The voice was soft. The smell was floral. He lifted his eyes to look into the familiar grey-blue eyes, but... black, gleaming eyes held his. Long hairy arms...

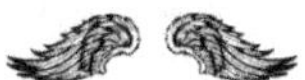

RIPPING THE PILLOW from his face, he blinked. *Light...* he must have light. Was he going mad? He needed to escape, but how did he escape his own mind? The brown curtains chinked open and light crept across the horizon. Awake, he found the smoke he'd crafted the night before and stuck it in his pocket. He pulled on his old shoes, splashed water on his face and drenched his hair, making it behave.

At the door, he turned back and put the rest of his new stock in the tin. With it safely hidden, he retrieved the Bible from the floor.

God's book. He could hear his grandmother's voice. 'Okay, God. What have You got to say to me today?' He flicked the pages, threw it into the air, caught it behind his back and opened it at random. With his eyes closed, he pointed to the page.

'*He said, "I am the light of the world. Whoever follows Me will never walk in darkness..."*'

He dropped the book, ran from the room, slamming the door behind him. He ran as though he was still dreaming, ran until his legs burned and his lungs were about to explode. Ran through the early morning light, watching as light chased darkness, until the only place the darkness could survive was in the alleyways, the deep bushes, the hidden corners.

In one of those corners, he sold the rolled drug for a good price. He ran past Maccas, Woolies, and into a coffee shop boasting a sign, *He Brews*. In a chair, on the footpath, he waited for his cappuccino and watched the sun change the colour of the world. He'd never noticed light before. Day and night. They come, they go. But never had the night been so dark, or the light been so welcome. What did it mean? Who claimed to be the light of the world? Surely the sun was the light of the world. There was no darkness when the sun was up.

'Enjoy your coffee, mate.' The young guy wasn't a lot older than Dan. He picked up the number from Dan's table. 'Is there anything else I can get for you?'

'Permanent light. No more darkness.' Dan listened with horror as the words came out of his mouth. They were irretrievable.

'I'll check the menu for you. "No more darkness."' He grinned at Dan and disappeared through the door.

As the sun crept higher, the horror of the night retreated in Dan's mind. It was only a dream, a nightmare. He must get a grip on himself. It was his emotions running away with him. No more emotions. No more thinking. From now on he would push toward his goal. Education. Good money and then he would build a family of his own. Amalya's cheeky grin floated in front of his eyes, her long brown hair swaying in the breeze.

'No more darkness.' The young guy dropped a plate in front of Dan. A pile of pancakes was topped with a sunny egg. Maple syrup formed rays, leading out from the sun.

El Roi

Chapter 7

'Hey mate.' The guy called from across the street as Dan left *He Brews*. Dan turned and the man beckoned him over. A couple of cars whizzed past giving Dan enough time to assess the bloke. Why would he single him out? Was he a client? He was older than the young blokes that played on the edge of drugs. The ones who usually stopped him.

The last car crept past as the driver looked for an address. Now Dan had no reason not to respond. 'You called me?'

'Yeah. Want to go for a walk. Bit noisy here.' His clothes were shaggy, his hair looked messy, but not dirty. His eyes avoided Dan's.

A caution siren blared in Dan's head, but he nodded and fell into step beside the guy.

'You live around here?'

'Could do. And you?'

'Close enough. I hang out around here a bit.' The guy, who hadn't introduced himself, turned into a park and followed the path which led through a clump of dense flowering bushes.

The perfume reminded Dan of soft grey-blue eyes. 'What do you want with me, mate? I need to get home.'

'I've heard you stock foul minis.'

'Foul minis?' Dan's tummy flipped. He was sure now the bloke was an undercover cop. *Careful. Don't give him any reason to search you.*

'Or was it Bible minis?'

'What are minis and why are you asking me?' *Calm yourself, Dan, or he'll read it in your face.* The guy's eyes were focused on him now. Clear. No sign of the drugs his clothes were trying to portray. Dan turned into a path leading to a kids'playground. No longer alone, but surrounded by kids and mums, he relaxed a little.

He flopped onto a bench seat and waited. The guy sat beside him. 'Good to see kids playing.'

'Don't like it myself, but you're freaking me out so any people seemed good.'

'Sorry, mate. I thought you could help me.' The man stood and strode away—the stride of someone who had another assignment to go to, not an aimless druggie.

A ball shot towards him. Without thinking, he caught it in his left hand and tossed it back to a little kid. The action seemed to pop his brain into gear. He jumped up and followed the cop, from a distance, heart still racing. He trailed the guy for about three blocks, keeping out of sight. Then he was picked up by a white Commodore.

Dan's legs turned to jelly. The cops were onto him. Now his hands began to shake and his heart hammered blood through his temple. Again he ran—ran for home. No one waiting for him, but still his only safe place.

El Roi

'Hey, Dan? The devil on your back?'

He stopped and looked around. Two guys from school sat in a car near the gutter. They were mini users, decent blokes.

'No. The pigs.'

'Where?' The guys looked down the street. 'Hop in. We'll get you away.'

'Nah. They've gone now.'

'We were hoping to see you. Need stock for a party tonight.'

'I'm out of business. Too dangerous.'

'But you've got the goods. What will you do with it?'

'Dump it.'

'Dump it with us... please...'

Dan paused. Were they being watched? But this was a sale, an offer of his last sale. Or he could just dump it and tell them where to find it. As his brain fought with itself, the guy nearest the window shoved the last bit of burger into his mouth. He balled the wrapper and added it to a Maccas bag.

Leaning past Dan, he threw it towards a bin on the footpath. It missed.

'Lousy shot.' Dan picked it up and backed six paces and threw. As the bag sailed toward his target, he knew what to do. When it missed, the guys roared laughing.

'I'll need a Maccas takeaway and one hundred and fifty bucks. Meet me there in three hours, and I'll tell you where I've dumped the goods.'

'One hundred...' countered the driver.

'Nup.' Dan shook his head, picked up the Maccas bag and walked away.

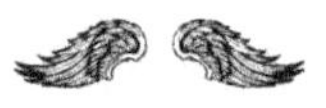

He rinsed the *Ready Remedy* tin three times and flushed the contents. Jack next door looked surprised when he asked for a loan of a broom, but gave it to him, chatting at the door while Dan swept the floor. He'd shaken out his bed sheets and all his clothes. His dirty clothes were bagged ready for the laundromat. He swept the dirt from the floor onto a sheet of the free newspaper that littered the footpath every week.

The broom? What if there were traces of anything on the broom? Before Jack could stop him, it was dunked in the sink.

Jack stepped into the room. 'Why'd you do that?'

'Mum always washed her broom. Don't you wash yours?' Dan peered into the sink. 'I can tell. Water looks like Kedron Brook on a bad day.' He rubbed it under the tap with his hand, careful to make sure there would be no splashes.

'There. Clean as a whistle.' He pushed out the door and tipped it upside down in the sun. 'Thanks, Jack, for your help. This place needed a good clean.'

'And you reckon my broom was dirty. All your muck, I reckon.' He turned and went home, much to Dan's relief. Time was running out. On his hands and knees, he wiped the floor with wet toilet paper. It flushed easily.

His cargo waited at the door, in a bag of rubbish. He dropped it in a bin just before Maccas.

'We got a Big Mac, is that ok?' The guys leaned on the wall near the door.

Dan slid into a booth. 'Sounds wonderful. I'm hungry.' Each of the guys took out a burgers and chips. They passed the bag to Dan. After he'd grabbed his burger and chips, the bag was empty except for three fifty-dollar bills.

El Roi

'The big burger has been dumped in the bin in yonder park, still in the takeaway bag.'

'It better be as you say.' The guys were jittering as though they'd already smoked the stuff.

Dan chomped into his burger. 'You'd do well to trust me until you get home. The cheeseburger has the lot. Thanks for my lunch. I appreciate it.'

In a corner booth he transferred the cash to his wallet, telling himself to keep it towards a smart phone. But it was heavy. What if the cops found him with so much cash? Woolworths was over the road. He needed a broom and toilet paper. And food.

When the white car stopped him an hour later, he had supermarket bags balanced on each end of a broom that he carried on his shoulder. In his wallet was a fifty dollar Woolworths voucher, twenty dollars and enough coin to operate the laundromat for a month.

'Dan Furley.' A uniformed policeman with a potbelly climbed out of the car. 'We need some help with our inquiries. Hop in and we'll give you a lift home.'

'How do you know my name?'

'A few inquiries.' His voice was polite, but it carried the veiled threat of his father's tone. 'You want to hop in, or I could do a drug search here?' He opened the back door.

Dan sat beside his groceries, with a broom for company. A metal grille separated him from the old codger and the sharp-chinned female driver. His pulse hammered in his temple. *Cool it, Dan.* But he could handle anything except the copper's tone. His body started to shake as visions of his angry father filled his mind. He leaned back into a corner, left arm over his face and waited for the familiar pain to explode.

The car stopped. The front door opened... and then his door.

'Okay, let's go check the house first.'

There was no arguing with the voice or the hand that grabbed his arm. Dan slid out of the car and opened his eyes. 'But...'

'No buts, son. It will go better for you if you cooperate and unlock the door.'

'I don't live here anymore.'

'Since when?'

'The school reported Dad for bashing me. Social workers moved me out. Dad's left town anyway.'

'Where do you live now?'

Dan gave his address and climbed back in the car, looking over his shoulder. The old place looked different. A plant with red flowers stood where Dad's dirty work boots used to be. Maybe he needed a plant? It looked more like family than it used to.

They drove past the end of Red Fred's street. What if they'd arrested him? Dan sank back down in the seat. What if they put him in jail? There was no one even to ring. No one to pay bail.

Head down, he led them down the path past the watchful eyes of the old lady and Jack. Heat raced up his neck. Jitters danced in his belly. His hand shook as he turned the key and stood back to let them enter.

He shut the door against neighbours' eyes and leaned on it. The policewoman disappeared into his bathroom. The belly worked his way around the mess going from left to right.

 El Roi

'Sorry it's so messy. Guess I'm not good at cleaning. Tried to do a bit this morning.' The guy ignored him and kept moving things to one side.

'What's in the bag?'

'Washing. Would you like me to tip it out? It's smelly, though. I just got coins this morning to work the laundry.' Talking seemed to calm him even if neither copper bothered to listen. The lady came out of the bathroom and moved to the kitchen. She picked up something from the bench. 'What's this? Why have you got Rodger's card? Aren't you sixteen? Too old for his department?'

'He gave it to me. He said I could ring him any time. Asked me to his youth group. I might go.' He moved closer to the woman and saw her face for the first time. Her chin was sharp, her nose pointy and her eyebrows flat. But her eyes were kind.

She passed the card to Dan. 'Better put it in your wallet in case you need it. If you have any drugs, believe me you will need it. When did you last smoke?'

Dan took the card and met the woman's eyes. 'Thanks. And I don't smoke. I never have until Jack next door gave me one yesterday. Nearly choked to death on the first draw.'

'I wasn't talking about tobacco.' She picked up his bin and tipped the contents on to the floor.

'Hey, kid. What's this?' The big copper's voice made Dan quake. He turned to see the policeman holding the little red Bible.

'My... my Bible.'

'There's pages cut out.'

'Don't like everything it says.'

Jo Wanmer

'Exhibit A.' He dropped it into a clip-lock bag.

'Are you going to keep it? I need it.' Why'd he say that? Suddenly he wanted to read more about the light... he was scared of the dark.

'Do the lights stay on at night in jail?' Did those words come out of his mouth?

Both coppers stopped what they were doing and looked at him.

She spoke first. 'There is always some light. Are you expecting to be in jail, Dan?'

'You've got me. Isn't that what you do?'

'We are only following a lead. Maybe we should just save everyone time. Where are your drugs hidden, Dan?'

'I don't have any.'

'Our sources say you do and you roll them in Bible paper.'

'Only an idiot gets caught in drugs.' Or the desperate, the lonely, the sad... he managed to keep the words in his head.

'Are you an idiot, Dan?' The policewoman turned him to look at her.

'No, Ma'am. I'm not an idiot... I'm quite smart. Desperate, lonely, sad...'

She patted his shoulder and turned to her colleague. 'I haven't found anything. Shall we follow the next lead?'

With a groan, potbelly straightened from searching through dirty clothes. 'We'll go, but he's coming with us. He's not an idiot and he knows more than he's saying. Let's see how much he talks after a night in a cell in the dark.' He walked to the door. 'In the car, Dan. When I get to the station I want a full statement from you.'

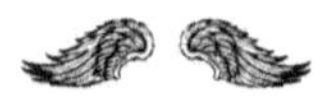

     El Roi

A FEW HOURS LATER Dan curled on his side on the carpet of the interview room. They'd searched him... searched parts of his body he would have never thought to hide drugs. Then they told him to wait in this room. He'd rather take a beating from Dad than this. Shaking, he curled into a ball below the window so they couldn't watch him. He tried to stop the tears but he was tired. The day started with monsters and finished with monsters. It'd been a long day. He'd moved from being a dealer to walking straight... just in time. He'd cleaned his room, only to have it destroyed by the coppers. The dream floated in front of his eyes. Perhaps he would be better sleeping here... polite human monsters or hairy long-legged creatures...

'Dan. Get up. Tell me who supplies your drugs. Now!' Dan pushed up, out of a deep sleep. The copper nudged him with his toe. 'C'mon! Where do you get your drugs from?'

Dad's tone, Dad's voice. Dan knew not to respond. He curled in a ball and covered his face with his left hand, protecting his writing hand. He had to write to learn. He had to learn.

'Stop it!' The woman's voice broke in. He heard them leave and the door click shut.

Awake now, he calmed himself. He pulled his t-shirt off and wiped his face, being careful to use the inside as his mother had taught him. He pushed his hair back, running his fingers through tangles. His pressing problem was his need of a toilet, or even a pot plant. No, he really needed a toilet.

He knocked on the door and tried the handle. It opened. There was no one in the hall, but no toilet sign either. He ran down the hall.

'Hey, you! Come back.'

He turned. 'Toilet... please.'

'Next door down. I'll wait.'

A young constable with cropped red hair waited outside the toilet door. 'What are you doing running in the police station?'

'I only just made it, man. Can you take me back to my room?'

As they walked along the hall, they met the potbelly. 'You can go, Furley.' He gave him his Bible and wallet and turned to the young constable. 'You can show him out.'

Darkness was descending, but the buildings still glowed in the soft pink of sunset. Dan stood and looked up and down the street. His unit was three blocks if he turned right. The shops and takeaways were half a block to the left. Neither felt good. A police car sped out of the drive beside the station, turned left and roared down the street, lights flashing, sirens blaring. One thing he did know. He never wanted to be in a police car again. And he never wanted to be in the dark again. But darkness was inevitable. It came like clockwork unless he stayed in the light.

He turned to the right and plodded down the street. He'd bought food but he was hungry. The pink light was fading to purple. Shadows had never bothered him before but now they hid the unknown. Leaving the main road, he followed a side street. Two blocks on this road. Left into his street and half a block down. He started to jog. This street was badly lit and purple was deepening into black. His heart seemed to race faster as the light dimmed further. He sprinted to the next street light and loitered past. But in the light, he could be seen by whatever was hidden in the dark. The pulse in his neck was deafening. He wiped the sweat off his palms and down his pants, ignoring his mother's voice in his conscience.

El Roi

Shadows moved in the street in front of him. People. But who? The not-quite-dark hid defining features. Were they safe or unsafe? Hairy monsters gloated before his eyes. He turned and ran. Pumped his legs like pistons. Back to the main road, past the police station, the shops, the takeaways.

No more darkness. That's what he wanted. *I am the light. I am the light. In me there is no darkness.* The road led past a park. It was full of shadows and movements, but the road had traffic and cars had lights. He ran beside the gutter, close to light. Visible.

Two more corners and he stopped in the soft light in front of *He Brews*. The joint was pumping. People were everywhere. He pulled back into the shadows that, here, seemed safer than the light. *Dan, you're losing it, man. Get a grip.* He looked around. Over the road, light fell out of windows, highlighting plastic mannequins wearing long fancy dresses.

Darting between cars, he sat on the ground, to the side of the pool of light and watched the activity over the road. Young men and women dressed in black ran from table to table, delivering food or scooping up armfuls of dirty dishes. Most of those who left tables wandered through double glass doors beside the coffee shop and disappeared inside. Kids came from everywhere, cars stopped and off-loaded kids. They all went through the double doors, laughing, joking, calling out to each other. It reminded Dan of school just before the bell.

By the time there were spare tables at *He Brews* Dan's stomach was rumbling. He crossed and found a little table close to the door, behind a sandwich board. A waiter skidded to a stop. 'Cook not taking orders soon, so what would you like?' The guy stopped and looked at him. 'I know you. You want *No More Darkness*, right?'

Dan shook his head. 'Um... I do.'

The waiter laughed and rushed toward the kitchen. Dan hoped he heard his belated yell for coffee. A few people still ate. Waitresses were hanging up their aprons and chatting together. Others cleared tables at speed.

His coffee arrived first, too hot to drink but wonderful to smell. The knot in his stomach started to unravel. A plate landed in front of him. 'Don't be too long. It's about to start.'

Dan stared. The plate was a sun, a pile of yellow Corn Chips, laid in such away the edges were pointy like sun rays. The middle dripped with melted cheese, highlighted by edges of green. He sipped his hot coffee, wondered how to eat such a creation and what the waiter meant. What was about to start? Where had the people gone?

The evening version of *No More Darkness* tasted better than the morning version. Dan was only halfway through when the waiter returned looking for his empty plate. 'You're not finished? You can't take it in, but I can slide it onto a takeaway so I can lock up.'

His food was whisked away and returned a few minutes later in a white box. 'You coming in, man?'

'Where?'

'Youth concert tonight. Everyone's excited.' The waiter untied his apron and looked at Dan. 'Oh. Haven't you been before? First time it is free. Come with me and I'll fix it.'

With the box of food under his arm, he was rushed through the double glass doors and into a large, darkened hall. 'This way, man. They're about to start.'

 El Roi

The place was packed. Dan couldn't see a spare chair anywhere but he followed his guide down the side aisle to the front row. After a whispered conversation with a man in the front row, the waiter waved Dan to an empty seat and ran back. Every eye in the hall seemed to be on him. He slid down into the chair. The girl beside him whispered to her neighbour. The bloke on the other side was older and well-dressed. Dan squirmed. He was wearing cheap surf shorts and shirt. His half-eaten dinner shone like a neon light in its white box. Although still hungry he wasn't game to eat.

Get out of here, Dan! But the only way out was past a million eyes. He scanned the hall, looking for other exits. The lights in the house went out. Spotlights swept over the stage. Four men and a girl ran out and loud music reverberated, filling every space.

The hall came alive. Some danced, some ran to the front, everyone joined the song. Dan watched from his chair, white box filling his hands. His eyes darted from two guitarists strumming to black fingers flying over a keyboard and the expressionless bearded face on the guy plucking a bass guitar. But a tiny woman, blonde curls jumping with the beat, belting drums and cymbals grabbed his attention. Energy, excitement and laughter radiated from her.

Lights spun over the hall, spotlighting him for a nanosecond and plunging him back into darkness except for the reflection from the stage. The darkness was safe here... as though there was light in it. As the second song started, Dan stood with the mass of kids and danced. He hoped it would never end. He could dance his life away in this light dark, or dark light. Whichever way it happened to be didn't matter. He loved it.

Sweat dripped off his chin onto the floor and still he danced. His throat was sore from yelling, but still he sang until it stopped. Just stopped. Everything hushed. Youth rushed to find seats. He wanted to scream. *Don't stop. Please, I want the music to go on and on and on.* Turning, he realised he was the only one standing. Then someone laughed... another joined in... then the hall erupted in hilarious laughter. Were they laughing at him? He was the only one left standing. They must be laughing at him. He fled, leaving the white box under his chair.

'Dan... Dan Furley. Stop!'

He was in the street, the dark street and halfway to the corner when he heard the call. He slowed and looked over his shoulder.

'Dan… please... wait up.'

Rodger? Was it Rodger? He stopped and turned, puffing, sweating.

Rodger raced up, gasping for air. 'Dan! I was so excited to see you but you took off as though a tiger was chasing you.'

'They laughed at me.' He strode toward the corner.

'Who?' Rodger touched his arm. 'Oh! I get it. No one was laughing at you. They were just laughing for joy.'

'Can you do that?'

'Sure can. Want to come back in with me?'

'No... I think I'll get home while it's still light.' The words were out before he realised how crazy they were. Rodger stood looking at him with one eyebrow raised.

El Roi

'Light?' The streets were dark except for the pool of light under each street lamp. Dan shuffled his feet. 'There was light in there and no darkness, even though it looked dark. I need to get home while there's still light clinging to me.'

For the third time that day, he ran through the streets as though his father was on his tail.

Chapter 8

His body was exhausted. His insides were buzzing. His head puzzled. Unable to sit still, he picked up the pile of dirty clothes and stuffed them into the garbage bag. The harsh light from the fluorescent tube highlighted his mess. With one sweep of his arm, his bed was clear. He kicked off his clothes, scoffed a can of cold beans and fell onto the bed. His body was sticky, sweaty so he pulled himself up and stood in the shower.

'He washes me, washes me clean. No mark left. Spotless I am.'

Dan had sung the song with the band. He sang it now in the shower. Over and over until he was so tired he turned off the light and fell into bed and dreamed.

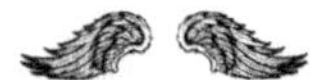

Amalya was playing the drums, shining brown hair flying, head bopping, hands moving so fast they were a blur. He danced to the rhythm, clapping his hands, stomping his feet. She saw him and laughed, clanging the giant cymbal at the same time.

Her eyes called him to come. Her laugh cascaded over him. He danced toward her, but he couldn't get there. An invisible glass wall separated them. Running to the right and left, he tried again, but every time the barrier stopped him.

Mocking laughter filled his ears, drowning out the wonderful beat of the drums. He spun behind him. The monsters were closing in. Like hyenas they moved, prowling, snivelling, slobbering. His back was against the wall, invisible but impassable. He turned back to Amalya. She was shrugging as if to say, why aren't you coming?

He spun back. The monsters were almost on him. Gloating, salivating, shoulder to shoulder.

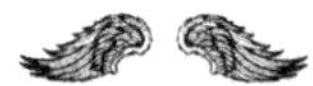

HE WOKE SHAKING. His heart raced in his chest. The light, he needed the light. Standing, he moved toward the switch, but in the inky darkness hairy arms and legs waved towards him. There was no way to the light switch. He pulled back into the corner, shaking on his bed, terror crawling like giant ants up his throat, threatening to block all air.

He gasped, but they drew closer and closer. Like the dream, they mocked and muttered. More aware now, fight rose up within Dan. 'Get out.' It was more a squeak than a voice.

Their steps faltered and they moved sideways, back and forth.

'Get out, now.' His voice was still weak but audible.

They growled but stopped. *You can't tell us what to do.*

El Roi

Schoolyard bullies. That's what they were. If they'd sounded like his dad he knew his quivering body would have caved. But they didn't.

Dan jumped, landing on the floor with a bang. 'Get out now.' He rushed to the wall and flicked the light switch. Nothing. No one. Just a strange dirty smell. Sliding down the wall, he shook, waiting for the pulse to stop banging in his neck. Did he dream all of it? Why were they coming? What were they? He wanted to cry, but one never cried in front of a schoolyard bully. Now they were in his bedroom, or maybe they had gone. The only way to know was to turn the light out—and he wasn't doing that ever again.

If he lay on his back, the light assaulted his eyes. On his side with his back to the light, he tried to doze but the brightly lit room pulled him back to consciousness. On his back, pillow pulled tight over his head and eyes shut tight, he started to relax but images of advancing shadows jolted him awake.

Restlessness drove him to the sink for water. *Coffee.* He boiled his shiny silver jug, spooned a small amount of granules and added milk. The hot beverage calmed him a little. His little red Bible lay on the floor near his feet. On the end of his bed, near the open window, he sipped coffee and opened it at random.

'Our Father in heaven...'

There's a father in heaven? Dan shuddered. Whose father? His father wasn't there. One thing he knew; he wasn't going to heaven if he had a father there. He read on. '...hallowed be Your name.'

Dropping the Bible, he gulped hot coffee. It didn't even make sense. Why was his grandmother so fond of the book?

He preferred a God who claimed to be the light of the world, rather than anyone's father. How he could he find more about light? He needed light. The darkness was freaking him out. Flicking through the book, he looked for light, reading bits here and there.

Jesus went up the mountain to pray... why would he do such a thing?

The disciples started to argue... Well, that sounds normal.

The herd of pigs ran down the slope, into the sea and they all drowned.

Dan sipped his coffee. This story sounded better. He started at the top of the page. It talked of a crazy guy, living among the graves. Everyone was scared of him. Jesus told demons to leave and they went into the pigs and drowned them.

Demons?

Was it demons chasing him? All he knew about demons was his grandmother talking about 'that demon drink.' She used to make the comment when dad was drinking rum. He shuddered. It sure sent him wild. But... Jesus told them to go, to get out. Could anyone tell them to go?

He longed for morning, for light. As soon as the sun came up, he was going to bed to sleep. If those monsters were coming in the night, he'd sleep in the day and stand guard at night. Picking up the red book, he turned more pages, hoping he'd find another story.

The lost son. Interesting! Was he a lost son? More like he'd lost his parents. He lifted his cup, but it was empty. Might as well read another story.

One son demanded money and the father gave it to him. Dan laughed. This was obviously a fairy story. He read on. The

 El Roi

son took off and spent all his money. What a fool. It made him angry. There was a kid whose father gave him a great start in life and he wasted it.

Dan put the book down and boiled the jug again. Now if he had a lot of money, he'd get good stuff. A computer, or even buy a computer shop if there was enough. Buy and sell. Make more money. Make sure it never runs out. But not the guy in the story. Broke, eating out of a pig trough. Dan knew what it was like to have nothing to eat. What would this idiot do?

Dan balanced his hot mug to read further. The guy went back to his father, begging and pleading. Dan would never do that. *Never.* Go back to his father with his tail between his legs? He'd rather starve. It would be better than being bashed to death when his father found out he'd wasted his money.

The sky was lighter, starting to change colour. He leaned on the window sill and watched the transformation. Light changed everything. Wide awake, he grabbed his washing and wallet and headed to the laundry.

The clothes turned over in the drying machine like his thoughts tumbled through his brain, confused and jumbled together. He wished he had someone to talk to, but his school mates would think he'd lost his senses. Gangly hairy monsters and weird stories weren't the normal conversation topics.

Rodger! But he'd run away from Rodger last night. Why was he there anyway? More questions to add to the jumble. The dryer stopped and he pulled everything out and shoved it into the black bag. Tiredness dogged him. Loneliness consumed him. Sadness confused him. He walked down past the old lady's unit. From her window she yelled to him. 'Happy Christmas, boy.'

He stopped and turned. 'What?'

'You only need a beard and you'd look like Santa Claus. You've got the white hair and the sack.' She chuckled.

'Christmas? Is… is it today?' The sadness settled heavily in the pit of his stomach, threatening to consume him.

'No! Two more days. It's on Thursday. Would you like to come to Mass with me on Wednesday night? You could walk with me and keep me safe.' Her eyes reflected his own loneliness. 'I asked my boy to take me but he's too busy. My daughter's in London, but she is going to ring at eight o'clock on Christmas morning.'

'What is Mass?'

'You don't know?' She sighed. 'I guess there are lots of young ones who don't know. It's in the church and we celebrate the birth of Jesus. You do know about that, don't you?'

Dan moved his load to the other shoulder. 'Um… of course.'

'Good. Are you busy Wednesday night? I'd like to go about ten if it's ok.' She beamed at him, head nodding up and down. 'Come in and I'll pour you a lemonade. You look hot. Have you had breakfast?'

Dan dropped the bag at the door and entered a room. It was the same as his, yet completely different. Every object looked as though it had been positioned exactly. Flowers, figurines, lace, photos, books and knickknacks filled every bench. In the corner was her bed, covered in fabric with flowers. On the floor were mats, also covered with flowers.

He accepted a cold glass of lemonade.

El Roi

'I usually eat two boiled eggs with soldiers. Would you like the same?' She filled a white saucepan with water. He craned his neck. Yes, it, too, had flowers.

The eggs were dropped into the saucepan. 'Is it your washing in the bag?'

'Yes. I've just finished it.'

'Did you fold it well? I hope you did or everything will crush.' She waved a spoon at him. 'Well?'

'Fold it?'

'Bring it here.' She patted her bed. 'Tip it out.'

With lots of tutting she sorted and folded clothes, smoothing them out on her bed. 'Where do you put them when you get home?'

'I've got one little set of drawers but they're full. They'll go on the floor.'

'They'll do no such thing!' She put eggs in flower cups in front of him on her table. 'Eat up. Then we will shop.'

Dan nearly choked. 'Where?'

'Cheap shop. C'mon, eat up.'

Two hours later a little set of plastic drawers held all his clothes. The whole room looked different but it didn't look like Christmas.

Christmas. He leaned against his door. Mum always decorated a plastic tree. There were presents. Chicken, ham and salad, and then ice cream. Dad got drunk. The day often ended in a fight but most days did. Even last year Dad bought ham, nuts and extra grog. But no one? Alone? He shut the ugly brown curtains and flopped on the bed. The sheets stank. Tomorrow he'd wash them. Clean sheets as a Christmas present. It wouldn't be the worst present he'd ever got. At least no worse than the year Dad got him a computer game when they didn't have a computer. But it wasn't presents he wanted. It was eyes. Soft, loving, understanding eyes. Proud, encouraging eyes like he saw Red Fred turn on Bazza. Amalya's adoring eyes. Maybe Mum would come. It was her eyes he longed for most. He allowed himself to cry until sleep claimed him.

He woke with a start. It was dim in the room. He flung back the curtains and the room flooded with light but it would be dark soon. A torch. Old Alice had dragged him to the cheap junk shop. There were all sorts of treasures in there. It was time to go shopping.

He tipped six Weetbix in a bowl and poured the last of the milk on them. They were Mrs Rhodes's idea and they were good.

When he ventured out his door, the sun was getting low in the sky. Dan figured he had a bit of time before it was dark. Past Woolies, he turned down the side street and into the crowded shop. Wandering down the aisles, he found three torches. He picked a black one. It wasn't too big so it would fit in his pocket. He added one with a strap. He bought an elephant night light as an early Christmas present. Some tinsel was on sale so he grabbed a couple of strands and two big bags of lollies. It might help it feel like Christmas. He looked at tools, pens, toys and weighed a cricket bat. He thought about another shirt, more shoes and a radio. He watched the pictures on the bank of TVs for a long time. A TV would bring life to the room, but he didn't have enough money. He was sitting on the floor in the book section when they flicked the lights and announced they were shutting the store in five minutes.

El Roi

It was dark. Dan stood outside the shop and stared up and down the street. A tremor ran the length of his spine. But he had a torch, one he could strap on his forehead. He stopped at a bench outside Woolies. Even they were closed and he was hungry. It took a while but he adjusted straps, inserted batteries and fitted the light. It had two settings. The bright setting lit the street like car headlights. The dull option would help while he slept.

His stomach rumbled so he jogged towards Maccas with his light off. No need to draw attention to himself where there was plenty of light. He paused just before he pushed the door. The joint was pumping with kids. About half of them he knew. They'd be complaining about home, or their job, or their dads. It annoyed him before he even heard it.

On impulse he turned on his light and jogged towards *He Brews*. He would order the same dinner. Grinning he followed his shaft of light through the dark.

Shut! It couldn't be. Every chair and table were stacked inside. Lights shone in the fridges but otherwise the place was deserted. Dan punched the wall. It hurt his hand but it helped to stop the flood of tears that welled in his gut. His safe place closed! Maybe the hall would be open. They all went there last night. But the doors were locked, only a faint light glowed from deep inside. Outside it now felt very dark, not the light dark of last night. Just dark, very dark. And he was a long way from his unit.

He sat on the floor, leaning on the glass doors trying to recapture the excitement of last night. But all he felt was reality of a dark street and deep loneliness. He trudged back the way he had come, hiding in the darkness, ready to flood his street with light if anyone came near, or if long hairy arms or legs appeared.

At home, he ate and then fitted the elephant night light into a power point on the bench. It filled the room with a soft glow. Yes, darkness couldn't chase the light. Satisfied the monsters were unable to appear, he slept.

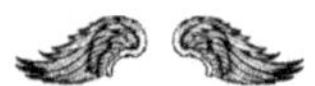

CHRISTMAS EVE. HE HATED IT but it was the truth. Bundling his sheets and the towel, he went to the laundry. There were people everywhere. He wasn't the only person who had promised himself clean clothes for Christmas. Leaving his bag in a corner, he went shopping. He needed ham. Maybe potato salad. And cherries. Not that he liked them but Mum always added them to the Christmas table and they looked good. In the cheap shop he bought a bunch of plastic flowers to give his neighbour, Alice. Warmth spread through his belly. He wandered the aisles and bought chocolate for Jack. He bought two more boxes of chocolates in case he saw someone else. Jumping in the air he clicked his heels. He could make it Christmas by giving other people things.

Then he saw her. A lady made of china, about as high as his hand span, dressed in a lavender and purple flowing dress. She looked like Mrs Rhodes and reminded him of his mother. He picked it up as though it was as delicate as his rollies. He put it back. There was no way he could get it to his mother, or Mrs Rhodes. When he was in the queue at the checkout, he counted his money. He had enough. Maybe he could bring it back in a few days and get his money back?

El Roi

The laundry had cleared so he loaded the washing machine and sat back to wait. The little china lady called to him from his bag. He sat with her on his knee. 'Rose. I'm naming you Rose, even though you are lavender. Mum would love you. She'd put you up high where no one could break you...'

The memory burst from a hidden vault. He could see it like yesterday. Dad yelling, mum talking in her quiet, wavering voice. 'But Alf. They didn't have any double-smoked ham, only triple-smoked.' Dad turned around and grabbed the lady, the tall white lady. 'No, Alf, no. She was my grandmother's!' But he hurled it at her. When she ducked it smashed against the door and shattered into a million pieces on the floor. After Dad stormed off, Dan tried to cuddle her sobbing frame, curled on the floor. Then he started picking up pieces. He could try to stick them together. They'd stuck her mirror together after Dad threw it.

Afterwards he always had a distorted face.

'Hey, you. When you're finished mooning over your dolly, your washing is finished.' A mean-looking bloke glared at him. 'You better run home, mummy's boy.'

Heat flushed up his neck. He stuffed the lady back in a bag, grabbed his washing and took off. He strode home, fury simmering in his gut. No one called him a "mummy's boy" and got away with it. At home he packed the food into his little fridge, placed Rose on top of his new plastic drawers, locked the door and stormed back to the laundry.

He kicked the door open, fists balled at his side. 'Who did you call a "mummy's boy"?'

The weedy guy dropped his paper and glared at him. 'What you gunna do about it, boy?'

'Shut your mouth!' Dan threw a punch. It landed on the guy's chin, knocking him back into the machines. Murder sparked in his eyes. Dan had seen that look before. He fled, the guy right behind him.

Dan didn't look back until he reached Maccas. There was no sign of him. 'Wimp!' Dan muttered. He shoved out his chest, walking the strut of the victor. As he marched past the window of a shop, he jerked to a stop. *Dad!* But it wasn't his father … it was him. Walking like his father. Scowling like his father. Horrified, he ran back to the laundry.

'I'm sorry, mate. I'm sorry. Here, hit me back. I'm sorry. I don't want to be like my dad...'

An old lady looked at him, blinking vague, confused eyes. The guy wasn't there.

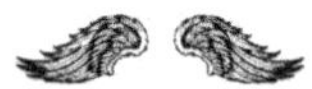

HE WANDERED THE STREET, telling himself he was looking for the guy to apologise. But he couldn't go back to his little room with this kind of chaos in his head. He had behaved just like his father. Was he going to be the same? If he wasn't, how did he know who to be?

'Dan! Hey, Dan.'

Who was calling him? Rodger ran back from his parked car. 'Busy? Want to drive with me for a bit?'

Dan nearly hugged him. 'Love to. Where are we going?'

'We are playing Santa Claus. Dropping off presents for our kids. Then if we're lucky you and I can grab a coffee. Why so glum, my friend?'

He decided not to tell him anything, but it all tumbled out in between stops anyway. After a couple of places, Dan took

 El Roi

the gifts to the door while Rodger found the next address.

Rodger pulled up near *He Brews*. 'All done but one. Time for coffee and I'm looking to eat. I haven't had lunch yet.'

The guy who took Dan to the concert stopped at their table. 'Rodger! Nachos and coffee?'

'Good call, mate. And the same for my friend.'

'*No More Darkness.*' The waiter winked and rushed away.

Rodger looked bemused. 'What did he mean? *No more darkness.* Last night you were making some excuse about light and dark. I'm confused.'

'*I'm* confused.'

'About what?'

'I read God is the light and in Him there is no darkness. I've been trying to work it out. There was light here the other night, even in the dark outside. But there's no light in my darkness. I had to buy a night light. The darkness didn't put it out.'

'Is the dark a problem?'

'It wasn't but...' Dan couldn't tell Rodger about monsters. He'd think he was a child.

'But...?'

'I had this dream. Now when it's dark these things chase me...' He shrugged. 'I feel like some kind of crybaby. Maybe that guy's right. I am a mummy's boy.'

The waiter returned. 'Two plates of *No More Darkness.*' He grinned at Dan and left.

'You must think I'm mad.' Dan twisted a corn chip out of the bottom of the stack and ate it, waiting.

Rodger followed suit. 'I think you're brilliant. This is the best plate of nachos I've ever tasted. The simple answer, Dan, is Jesus. He brings the light of the Father. With Him you'll never be in... '

'Did you say "Father"? I don't want anything to do with a father.' He jumped to his feet.

Rodger waved him down. 'Finish your lunch. It's fine.'

Twenty minutes later, Rodger pulled up at his gate and handed him the last parcel. 'Happy Christmas, Dan.'

'Wait...' Dan ran into his unit and grabbed one of the boxes of chocolates. He hadn't thought of wrapping! Embarrassed, he walked back to where Rodger waited, leaning on the car. 'Happy Christmas, Rodger.'

'Wow! You got this for me?'

Dan swallowed the lump in his throat. Rodger gave him a big hug and turned. 'Dan. God is a good Father. He loves you.' He jumped in the car, waved and roared down the road.

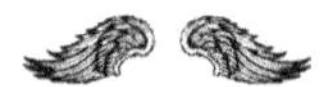

He made his bed the way his mother taught him when he was little. Everything would look good for Christmas. He even had a present, a red-wrapped box with a green ribbon. He shook it, turned it over, picked at the tape. No! He would wait till tomorrow. He sat it with the tinsel, chocolates and flowers on the table. He thought of adding Rose to the display, but instead took one piece of tinsel and wrapped it around her feet.

He stopped to admire his work, but pain squeezed his heart. There was no one to share his handiwork with, no one who cared. He grabbed the broom and started to sweep. He swept the walls, the floors, the outside path as though his

 El Roi

father was on his tail, but still the pain waited, as though ready to pounce as soon as he stopped.

'Hey, Dan.' Old Jack stumbled down from the street. 'Want a beer?'

'You're drunk, Jack.'

'You sound like my wife, bless her soul. She's gone to the big pub in the sky.' He opened his door and dumped a six-pack on his table. 'I've been toasting her. Here's to you, my love.' He pulled the lid on another bottle and slurped the golden liquid. It dribbled down his chin and onto his shirt. 'Help yourself, young Dan.'

'I... I gotta go home and finish cleaning. It's Christmas tomorrow.'

'Yeah. My son's coming to get me at ten. So I only got six more. Need to be sober for Christmas.'

Dan picked up the rest of the old guy's shopping and carried it in. One of the bags was dripping. He found ice cream, melted, and shoved it in the freezer. The milk he put in the fridge, leaving the rest in the bags on the table.

'You're a good boy, Dan.' Jack's words slurred. 'Your... your dad must be pr...proud o...' His head dropped onto the table.

'Jack.' Dan shook him. 'You should go to bed.' He pulled him up and together they stumbled across the room. Jack slumped into the bed. Dan lifted his feet and pulled off his shoes.

He slammed the door behind himself. Was that what a good son did? Put drunk men to bed? He'd done it plenty of times.

Angry, he stormed into his room and picked up Jack's chocolates. Why would he want to give them to a drunk old man? On impulse, he tucked them in his shirt and jogged to the station. He'd give them to Ginny as a thank you for a lovely meal. If he was lucky, he'd get another meal. He dodged the ticket guy and jumped onto the train. His wallet had enough money for a ticket, but he craved adventure.

Vaulting the fence at his old station he followed the familiar path to his childhood haunts. Fred's place was in the opposite direction to where they had lived, but he circled around past the shed where he first met Fred. Anger still boiled in his gut. *Good sons put drunks to bed.* Was that all he was worth? Was it the only way he'd ever belong? He was so desperate for relationship, any relationship, he was tempted to knock on the door of the shed. He grinned, remembering the adrenaline-jumping experience with those men. He missed the thrill of hiding hash, the challenge of sniffing out a sale and avoiding exposure.

For two days he'd gone straight and he was bored out of his brain. He'd done a great job of dodging the undercover cop and then he'd managed to clean up before they followed through. He high-fived the trunk of a palm tree. Yes, he'd proved he could survive.

The gate to the shed was down the next walkway. He jogged past it but there wasn't any action there tonight. Could he belong to that group? Belong there as part of a family? Maybe if he sold a different product he could fly under the radar. No more Bible wrapping. He needed a different angle.

He turned and headed to Fred's place, hoping he was home. Together they could plan. He ducked down a back street that would come out beside Fred's, and give him a chance to case it out a bit, see who was there.

At the corner a police car did a U-turn and stopped in front of the house. Dan ducked behind a shrub on the footpath,

El Roi

heart banging in his chest. Where he hid, he couldn't be seen, but neither could he see what was happening. He turned and retraced his steps. Fear of being seen and the need to know what was happening fought in his gut. His inquisitive nature won the battle, tempered by the fear. He circled to a park about a block from the house.

With the chocolates down his shirt, he swung his body up a tree. Hidden amongst the leaves, he felt confident he couldn't be seen. Police walked in and out of the house. A couple of officers searched the van. He couldn't tell what was happening but his gut contracted. Obviously the coppers were on to Fred. He ripped open the chocolates and devoured them, one after the other, trying to placate the growl in his belly. Poor Ginny must be upset but a box of chocolates wasn't going to help her.

News vans started to circle.

The light faded. Why hadn't he brought his torch? He wanted to get back to the light but needed to know what was going to happen. It was dark before they dragged Fred from the house. A coat covered his head but Dan knew it was him. The front door slammed shut as flash bulbs lit the area. He clung to the tree, stomach turning, body shaking, tears running down his face. Fred was a good man. They couldn't take him away at Christmas.

All Dan's emotions blended into anger. He'd go and stop those coppers taking his friend away. He swung down the tree and stormed down the road. The police cars accelerated away from him. As they moved, a cameraman moved to the side of the house. Through the window, Dan saw Ginny, doubled up on the floor crying beside a bare Christmas tree. The curtains swung shut. The lights dimmed. The cameraman shrugged and left. Dan crept in behind Fred's van, waiting. Dark was deep both inside him and outside.

'I want my daddy.' The wail was muffled but clear in Dan's ears. Loud sobs intensified. *Ginny.* The beautiful soft woman was broken. He raced to the back door. He needed to comfort her. But how? He couldn't bring him back, he couldn't hug the kids, he couldn't fix it.

He jogged from streetlight to streetlight, angry again. Angry with Fred. How could he do that to Ginny? *Drugs.* All his emotion focused on the deceptive weed. Never again would he have anything to do with it.

El Roi

Chapter 9

HE WAS NEARING the station when a black twin cab ute passed him and skidded to a stop.

'Dan!'

Dad! He froze. His brain said run, but his body stopped working as it always did when his father yelled his name.

'Dan. It's wonderful to see you, son.' His father raced down the footpath and slapped him on the shoulder. 'Hop in the truck. There's someone I want you to meet. I've been searching everywhere for you.'

Back at the truck, Alf pulled open the passenger door. 'Dan, meet your new mother. This is Felicity.'

Cool eyes sized him up as she slid over to make room for him. Curly red hair rioted around her face, flowing over her shoulders. Her mouth was orange. Her perfume, overpowering.

'Hi, spunky. I've heard a lot about you.' She patted the seat. 'Get in. We've spent hours trying to track you down.'

Dan stepped back. She purred like a cat but had the eyes of a tiger.

Alf pushed him from behind. 'Get in, Dan. We're going home. We came to spend Christmas with you.'

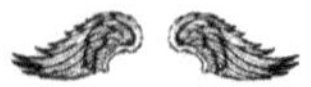

Felicity spun at the door of Dan's flat and glared at his dad. 'Alf! We can't stay here!'

'I didn't know… I thought he'd have at least got a decent unit…' He pushed past Felicity and glanced around the room. 'Aw, come now, girl. It's okay. At least it's clean.'

'There is only one bed and it's a single!'

Alf pulled her close and pinched her bottom. 'That's fine. We'll fit in one bed.'

The red curls flounced away. 'Only if you get lucky. Otherwise you'll be on the floor, bonding with spunky here.' She ran one fingernail from the tip of Dan's ear and down through his hair, though her eyes never left Alf's face.

Electricity shot from Dan's neck to his groin. He pulled back, confused. 'But… but you can't stay here… it's too small… I'm not allowed to have visitors…'

'Get over it, Dan. There're special exemptions for visitors over Christmas.' His father's tone closed the subject. 'Come. Help me with the luggage.'

When Dan returned, pulling a purple suitcase with two other bags balanced on top, Felicity was peering in the fridge.

'We'll need more food. There's not enough here to feed a sparrow.' She opened her bright orange mouth and dropped in two of Dan's precious cherries.

He wanted to object, but his father kicked open the door, silencing him.

 El Roi

'Lucky I still had the swag in the back, Dan.' He dropped it and kicked it across the room. It missed the new plastic drawers and landed in the corner. 'Clear this junk off the table, kid. There's nowhere to put anything.'

So much for his attempt at Christmas decorations. Dan grabbed his few presents and the string of tinsel, glancing round the room as his father headed out again. Not knowing what to do with them, he put them on the floor in the corner near the swag.

'What've you got there, spunky?' Felicity picked up the wrapped present. 'For me? How kind.'

'That one's mine.' Dan picked up the chocolates and offered them to her. 'These are for you.'

'Your father can have them. When he gets back. If I ate chocolates I'd lose this waistline.' She wiggled her body at Dan. Her waistline disappeared from his view behind a pink mountain of flesh. Dan dropped his eyes. His voice squeaked as he asked for the present.

'Finders keepers.' She started to pick at the ribbon. Dan's heart dropped. Rodger gave it to him. It may only be an orange or a bag of lollies but it was his. With a leap he snatched it from her.

Her green eyes sparked as she stalked towards him. 'Oh, I love a good fight. I should warn you I always win, and I don't feel the need to fight fair. What about you, spunky?' Dan was familiar with danger, but he'd never fought anyone like her. Yes, she would be unfair. Every nerve screamed a warning. He never let his eyes drop from hers, nor did he feel the need to answer her. One thing he was sure of. It was time to escape, but where to?

Backing away, he grabbed his backpack. It was his constant companion. The wrapped present went in with his torch, wallet and the few things he kept beside his bed. The red-haired tiger moved one of the two chairs in the room to the door side of the table. She reclined, holding the plastic flowers, Alice's gift, to her nose as though enjoying the perfume. Dan knew she was scheming as she watched, waiting, crouching. He shuddered and for the first time in his life, he hoped his father would return soon.

At the plastic drawers, he took out his newest clothes and wrapped Rose in them for protection. With a bit of maneuvering, he fitted everything in his bag.

'Going somewhere, spunky?' She leaned forward over the table pushing her body against her arms. Flesh popped out and up, soft and pink, overflowing in all directions.

Dan swallowed the lump in his throat. 'Think I'll just go and check on Dad.'

'He's gone shopping for a few things for me. He invited me, but I told him I wanted to get to know you better. Come over here and sit for a while.' Her eyes were a mixture of innocence and guile, but not soft… how he longed for soft eyes like Ginny's, but he couldn't think of Ginny.

Coffee. It might divert her so he could slip out the door. He went to the sink and filled the kettle. 'Would you like a coffee, Felicity? I should have offered you a drink earlier. I'm sorry.' He grabbed his mugs, glad he had followed Mrs Rhodes's instructions and bought two.

'Coffee? But darling, it's too late for coffee. We need something a little stronger.' She winked at him and placed a

El Roi

purple flask on the table. 'I always carry some for emergencies. Get the lemonade out of the fridge.'

'But the drink is…' Dan was silenced by glinting green eyes. The lemonade was for his Christmas dinner, but everything had changed, disappeared like the cherries.

He passed her the bottle and continued to make his coffee at the sink. Coming up behind him, she reached over him to get a glass. Then her other hand slid past his ear, reaching for a second glass. She pressed her body into his back. Her breath wafted around the base of his neck. She pushed further, as though she couldn't reach the glass, driving her pelvis into his bottom.

Crazy sensations exploded in his body. Every hair stood on end. He froze, waiting for her to retreat. He had to get out the door… anywhere… away… far, far away.

Glass in each hand, she lowered her arms so they slid over his shoulders, pushing his arms against his side. He dropped his coffee in the sink and watched the spilt brown fluid swirl down the plughole. His stomach swirled as her arms crossed over his chest and her body swayed behind his rigid back.

'C'mon, spunky. Dance with me to the table. We'll fill these glasses and drink together. I like you. You're sharp, much sharper than your dad.'

Somehow, the glasses reached the table, but the pressure in her arms continued to burn a cross into his chest. Was he breathing at all? He must have been but without moving a muscle. He'd outwitted the police, he'd fought off bullies, he'd kept his cool in a drug dealer's shed but this trap was one he'd never encountered. He stood, not knowing how to defend himself.

'Turn around, Dan.' Her whisper in his ear sent a shiver down his spine.

He turned to find himself jammed between her and the table, his legs like jelly and his tongue dry. Her lips locked on his, sending a plait of panic and pleasure coursing through his body. The tiger had trapped him.

A door banged open. 'DAN!' Before he could think or react, the toe of his father's boot belted into the side of his head. 'How dare you! I turn my back and you touch my wife?'

Felicity was dragged up and thrown towards the bed. Dan rolled across the room, trying to order his feet, his brain, his body. His head exploded with the familiar old fireworks from the boot kicking his temple. He scrambled to his hands and knees. His father's hand grabbed his hair, pulling up his head. Dan saw the fist coming. This fight he knew. He hadn't seen his father's eyes. Nor had the tone terrified him. Instinct kicked in.

Spinning away from the punch, he shook free and ran for the door.

'Get back here, now!' His father screamed in fury. But the intimidated, frightened son had changed. Dan bolted through the door and raced for the road. He was free. There was no way the old man could catch him.

Fire exploded in his back. Pain seared his body. *What's happened? Just keep running, Dan.* One more step … but he collapsed like jelly. Must get away… must get away. He tried to crawl but his face was planted into the dirt near Jack's doormat.

The click of the lock on Jack's door.

Heavy boots running.

Silence.

 El Roi

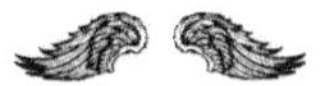

HIS BODY LAY FACE DOWN, crumpled. Blood, red blood, bubbled and flowed around a glinting handle. Dan watched from above as though disconnected. He was disconnected, hovering just above the roof. His body pulled at him, drawing him back. Another force sucked at him, dragging him away. Stretched like the rope in a tug of war, he saw hairy legs and leering faces, heard the gloating cackle, and the vile stench as the beings closed in on him.

He needed light.

Was anyone going to help him? The door of his unit banged open. Felicity stumbled out dragging her bags. His father followed. Surely Dad would help him.

'Alf, grab the purple bag. And get the knife.'

Dan watched as his father raced back inside. *But what about me, Dad? Are you going to help me?* Felicity raced to the car. His father ran along the walkway. He skidded to a stop at Dan's body. He *was* going to help him.

But Dad yanked the knife out of his back and raced toward the running car.

'Alf! C'mon. I can hear sirens.'

Tyres squealed.

Sirens approached.

Dad. What about me? Dan's body may be spread-eagled on the ground but looking from above, his soul's heart shattered. Dad didn't care. He'd left him in a pool of blood. The tug of war was over.

Dan accepted the pull from the sky.

No more pain. He was free. Faster and faster he travelled in a shaft, a clear shaft. But was he free, really? Gloating laughter surrounded him. Hideous faces leered at him. Terror pushed out the temporary euphoria. What was going on? Where was heaven?

Above him was light. Light beyond any light he'd ever experienced. He longed to be in it, immersed, enveloped, embraced… loved.

But cackling laughter pulled him away. Grotesque mocking faces and sharp-clawed talons reached out.

'DAN!' The sound reverberated around him. *Could it be…?* Everything paused.

'Oh, Dan.' The broken voice sounded like his mother.

Mocking, cackling laughter exploded around him. *His mummy. Too late! She can't help him now. He is ours, forever ours.*

Mum? He looked towards the fading light, trying to reach it. Had she finally come? Was she there? He tried to see back to his body. But a grotesque black creature marched towards him, flanked by black soldiers. The light was receding and there was nothing he could do about it. The mocking, sinister gloating swirled around him. Bullies… but too many of them. He decided to fight for the light, even if he died trying.

Died? The cackling and mocking reached a new crescendo, as though they could hear his thoughts. *Dead! Haha. You are dead. This is death, everlasting death. Hahahah…*

The light. He needed the light. This darkness had no light. Despair overwhelmed him. Darker than any darkness he'd ever known.

Jesus!

     El Roi

As the voice yelled, he jerked to a halt. The cacophony of noise ceased as though every demon held its breath.

JESUS! The cry bounced through the atmosphere. The demons shrieked and covered their ears.

'Dan! In Jesus' name, come back here. *NOW!'*

All progress ceased. A hush fell, as though all heaven and hell paused, holding its breath.

'Dan, I said, in Jesus' name, come back.'

The tug of war recommenced. The dark became light until the light extinguished the darkness. Light, light and more light. Until out of the light, a cloud of light—white, brilliant light approached him. Dan leaned toward it, hungry for it, desperate to be engulfed by it, to be hidden in the light.

···Dan. I am Jesus···

Jesus! Dan fell at his feet and held them. The light flooded through him, around him, in him. Light he could feel. A joy radiated through him. Tears of joy.

···We haven't met before, though you experienced My light at the concert···

Dan felt the words, rather than heard them. The concert when there was light in the darkness. Was that You?

···I've been drawing You to myself···

Why didn't someone tell me?

···Rodger tried···

Rodger had tried but he'd been so scared of the dark overcoming the light, he'd run.

Jesus, I'm sorry. Dan looked down at his clothes. They were dirty, filthy. Everything around was spotlessly clean. Jesus was pure. He pulled back from Jesus' feet. *I'm too dirty to be here.*

Two strong hands lifted him to his feet. Eyes so brilliant, overflowing with love, met his. Dan dropped his gaze.

Don't look at me! I'm filthy. Dan fell to the ground, curled into a ball, but even then he couldn't hide from the brilliance showing up every spot of sin. A soft cloud fell around him. Whiteness, but it seemed like blood. Whiteness covering his brokenness.

The hand lifted him again. *···My brother Rodger called to Me on your behalf. He's asking for your return···*

But I'm dead... well, that's what the demons said. And I'm dirty.

···In My Father's kingdom there is no death. I'm asking My Father for a second chance for you···

My father didn't try to even save me.

···But your Father in heaven is willing to save you, wants to save you. Look. You're wearing My cleanness... if you will accept it···

Dan looked at his hands. *Clean.* Looked at his body. *Clean.* Looked inside at his conscience. Everything was gone, washed, removed, leaving no sign of the regrets that had marked his life.

Your Father isn't like my father? It was only a thought, but he knew he was completely understood.

···My Father waits to meet you. He is not like your father, Dan. His love is perfect. Will you carry My light into the darkness? Will you go back?···

Dan, overwhelmed by the wonder of Jesus, tried to respond. *Will You come with me? I can't go alone.*

El Roi

…You will never be alone. My Spirit will be always with you. You can use one of His names, El Roi – the God who sees, to help you remember…

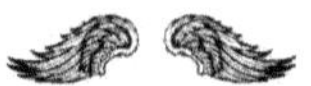

PAIN… excruciating pain… mind numbing, burning pain…

Chapter 10

WHITE LIGHT. HARSH, INVASIVE, angry white light. Dan tried to move, to cover his eyes but his body wouldn't respond. Even now, he couldn't control his choices.

The angry light flipped away, leaving a softer, less abrasive light. Dan tried to blink away the white spots in front of his eyes.

'Dan. Dan. Can you hear me?' The voice vibrated from a fuzzy shadow.

Was he dead or alive? He didn't know but he tried to nod. Pain shot through his head. Something filled his mouth, compressing his tongue. He gagged. His eyes shut in shock.

'He's still in too much pain. Lift the dose.' The light faded…

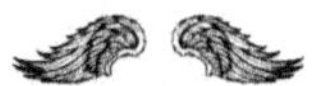

DULL LIGHT. SOFT LIGHT. Shadows. Red lights blinking. Rhythmic quiet beeping confirmed he was alive. No evil laughter. But no movement either. *Bring the light…*

'El Roi… El Roi…' It was more a mumble than a call. His throat was dry, scratchy. His tongue was free to move. 'El Roi.'

'He's awake!' A deep voice came from a shape leaning over him. 'Hi, Dan. It's good to see you. I'm your nurse. You've been critically ill but you're doing okay. You're in hospital.'

Bit by bit, the room came into focus. He blinked and the shape turned into a nurse… well, a guy with a moustache who acted like a nurse.

'Don't try to talk. Your throat is still recovering from a tube. Are you in any pain?'

Dan was lying on his side. His arms and legs were as inert as tree trunks. He felt peculiar but he shook his head. No pain. Wires covered his chest. Both arms had tubes attached.

'Can you squeeze my fingers for me? Push your foot against my hand. Can you see my finger? Follow it with your eyes.' Dan struggled. His eyes were tired but he followed the finger until it stopped in front of his nose. Exhausted, he closed his eyes. 'Good job, Dan. You're looking much better.'

He was too tired to care. What had happened to him? Crazy images of blood, hairy legs, and warm light fought for dominance. Nothing made sense. He dozed.

'Dan.'

His eyes flew open. *Mum? Here?*

Her familiar hand grabbed his, her lips kissed his cheek and hot tears dripped onto his neck. Mum was here. A lone tear escaped his eye. She brushed it aside with one finger, troubled eyes searching his. 'It's okay, buddy. It's okay now.'

He tried to squeeze her hand and was rewarded by a wet smile. 'You're awake. Thank you, God, he's awake.'

'Mum…' The rasp from his throat sounded like Mr Blueberry when he had laryngitis. 'Where did you go?' It hurt to talk. 'What happened to me?'

El Roi

His father's angry, bulging face flashed before him. Was Dad here too? Heart racing he scanned the room. What if he came? He must get somewhere safe. With a great effort he pushed himself onto one elbow.

The nurse jumped to his side. 'Dan. Lie still. I'll lift the bed a little. Try and make you more comfortable.'

'No… gotta go…' He struggled against the nurse for a second and collapsed back on the bed, gasping. The machines behind him beeped their dismay.

'Steady, mate. You can get up tomorrow, but not tonight.'

'But… Dad.' He tried to mask his fear, but his body trembled. The thought of his father scared him as much as the hideous long-legged monsters.

'Dan.' His mother stroked his head. 'Relax. Your father hasn't been here and I can make sure he isn't allowed in here.'

'How?' No one ever stopped his dad.

The nurse turned back, having silenced the beeping. 'Dan, in ICU every visitor is screened. I'll make sure your father can't get in. Rest easy, mate.'

His racing heart skipped a beat and slowed. He couldn't move. If Dad came he'd have no defence. 'How?'

In answer the nurse picked up a phone. 'Security. Alf Furley, Dan's father, is not allowed entry to ICU under any circumstances. By family request.'

Dan's breathing slowed. He'd never been this fearful before… but then he'd never been confined to bed before.

His mum wiped his forehead with a damp cloth. He had no idea how she found him, or why, but who cared? He just loved her being with him. He clung to her hand.

'Oh. My Jesus, my Jesus. Dan, did Alf do this to you?' Her voice broke. Her words muffled as her head buried into his chest. Her arms tried to find a way through tubes to hold him as she wept.

Dan's fuddled brain grappled with her question as he lay still, trying to gasp enough air. Dad could get very angry but surely he didn't do this. A memory hovered at the edge of his mind, as though blocked. Dad had been there. He'd kicked him. His hand touched the side of his temple. A bandage covering a lump confirmed the thought.

'Is it sore, Dan?' The nurse hovered over him.

'No. It's fine.' The familiar lie slipped from his mouth from habit. But this time it wasn't fine. He didn't even know if he'd recover… and why bother? Was there any point living for another fight?

'Light…' He closed his eyes against the intrusive light, longing for another strangely familiar yet unknown light. Welcoming and warm.

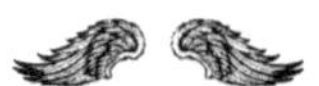

HE WOKE WITH A START. Dad was chasing him…. But he'd escaped… then…

But Mum was here. 'Mum. What happened to me? Where were you?'

She lifted her head and wiped her eyes. 'Dan?'

He'd woken her. 'What happened to me?'

'You were attacked, we think.'

In the dim light he saw his confusion reflected in his mother's eyes.

'Mum. I thought you were dead. Why did you leave me?'

 El Roi

'Oh, Dan, I'm so sorry. You're not the only one who's scared of your father. I ran to save my life. You weren't home. I left a note asking you to meet me. Why didn't you?'

'I didn't get a note.'

His mum's eyebrows shot into her hair. 'But then... then I got a message from you, saying you never wanted to see me again.'

Dan's mind was mush. He closed his eyes against the nightmare.

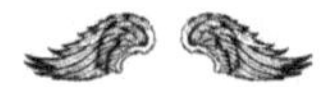

His Mum was still there when he woke. He drank from the straw the nurse offered him and clung to his mum's hand. 'I love you, Mum.'

She wiped her eyes. 'Your father fooled me. I'm sorry, Dan. I thought he'd look after you.'

'As if! But why am I so weak now? I've been in fights before, but never felt like this. What happened?' He pushed his head back on the pillow, gasping for air.

The moustache leaned over him. 'Easy, mate. Let your mum do the talking.' He studied something behind Dan. 'I'll increase the oxygen for a while. You need to rest.'

He wanted to argue. *Rest?* He hadn't done anything, yet every nerve end screamed. But he wanted to know, needed to know. 'Mum?'

Her hands—wonderful, familiar hands—held his. 'You close your eyes. I'll tell you what I know. When the paramedics arrived, you had a big hole in your back. Some old guy was pushing a towel on it to stop the blood... but...'

'How?' Ideas and images raced around his head but he couldn't order them.

'We don't know. The doctors say you were stabbed. The police are working on it.'

'You?'

She leaned in to hear him. 'Rodger tracked me down. He told me you wanted to see me. I was coming to see you for a Christmas surprise. We found you on the ground. The paramedics came and said you were dead…'

Dead? White light and hideous creatures fought for dominance. Confusion seemed to surround him. The dull pain in his back increased to a roar, shoving spears into his side.

'Time to sleep, Dan.'

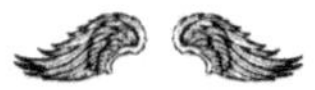

DAN WOKE FACING the other way. An old lady with hair pulled back into a bun was staring at the machines behind him. He had watched her for a while, trying to get his bearings. 'What day is it?'

She turned to smile at him. 'Sunday.'

Sunday? What day was it when Dad came? *Christmas Eve!* Of course. Mary… he was supposed to take Mary to church. 'Christmas?'

'You missed it.' She pulled up a chair and a wide grin lit her face, reaching all the way to sparkling eyes. 'But don't panic. Santa left your pressies here.' She squeezed his hand. 'In case you're wondering, you came in here on Christmas Eve night. Docs operated on you about ten o'clock and we've been making sure you're okay since. You slept Christmas Day and Boxing Day and woke yesterday. How're you feeling?'

El Roi

'It hurts to breathe.'

'Yup. That happens when someone throws a knife into your lung. Especially so low. You'll recover but only cause The Man Upstairs sent you back.'

Man Upstairs sent him back? *Carry the light… carry the light.* He pushed against the crazy ideas. 'I'm hungry.'

Her throaty chuckle comforted him. 'That's the best news I've had all day. Would you like orange juice or apple?'

As he sipped his drink, she sat and explained every wire and tube hanging off his bare chest and arms. When she explained the tube that came from between his legs, heat flushed his cheeks. He wondered who had put it in.

'All these bits will start to disappear now. You are much better today. We might even get you out onto a chair. With a bit of luck tomorrow you can go to a normal ward.'

'But Dad might come.'

'There are security guys everywhere. If he comes, press your call button. He'll be buzzed off like a bee. But now the police are waiting to talk to you. Are you up to it?'

'Why?' The old familiar fear pulsed through him. They took Fred. Were they after him?

'They are trying to work out what happened to you. They're on your side, Dan.'

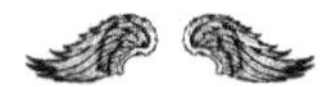

WHEN THE POLICEMEN walked in, Dan was sitting in an old lady's chair. Pillows propped him and protected a wound that wrapped around him from front to back. His mother leaned on his bed, her eyes weary and wary. The nurse behind him kept checking tubes and machines, patting his shoulder as though she could fix it all up.

'Thanks for seeing us, Dan.' The tall skinny guy in uniform had a gun halter strapped around his waist. He looked kind, but looks were deceptive. Dan tried to sharpen his wit, but his brain was sluggish. He must… must focus. 'My name is Detective Hilary. You can call me "Hill" if you like. This is Sergeant Allen.'

Dan nodded and waited, feeling like a bird near a trap.

'According to your doctor, your injury was likely caused by a knife thrust in your back and then dragged out. The person would have been behind you. Was someone chasing you?'

'Sorry.' Dan grappled with the information. 'I can't remember anything.'

'Can you remember what you did in the afternoon of Christmas Eve?'

'I shopped… but there was no one to have Christmas with. I was supposed to take Mary to church. I think I washed… or was it the day before…'

'Any visitors?'

He pushed his blond hair off his forehead and struggled to think. 'Dad came.'

His mum gasped but the policeman seemed unmoved. 'Does he come often?'

'Not since… not since the Family Services moved me. He's not supposed to come.'

'Were you expecting him?'

'Not likely. He found me in the street. Made me take him home. Said he came for Christmas. I argued… but Dad is Dad.' His memory was clearing now as though a dirty grey fog

El Roi

was receding. A slimy female face emerged out of the murky haze. 'Felicity.'

The word slipped across his tongue before he could check it, before he fully remembered. Heat flooded up his neck. He didn't even have a sheet to lessen his exposure.

'Who's Felicity?' A sharpened pencil point hovered between the raised eyebrows and the notebook.

'Red head.'

'Eyes?'

'Dangerous, green, slimy.'

'Slimy?' Sharp eyes seemed to see right into him.

Dan's skin crawled. It reminded him of the day the Year Eight girls had upended a bucket of slime on his head. But this time the slime was inside. He shuddered.

'You don't like her?' The second policeman was older, greyer and used the same voice as the sergeant who'd tried to get him for drugs.

Of course. He remembered now. Dad, using the same tone, yelling at him... angry. But this time he'd escaped... well, he thought he had.

'Dan?' The same voice again. He slid down in the chair, wanting to hide, to cower, but pain ripped through his back like a dagger. The nurse's arms were around him in an instant, holding him, lifting him.

'I'm sorry, gentlemen, but I think he's had enough for now. Maybe come back in a couple of hours.'

The detective stood. 'Sorry to tire you, Dan. So, Felicity gave you a rough time. Your dad's girlfriend?'

'Apparently my new... mother.' He choked, gasping for air. 'She's no mother.' He winced, his body threatened to break in two. The old nurse shooed the men away and laid back his old lady's chair. A needle slid into a port in his arm.

'Here, have some oxygen.' She fixed prongs into his nose. 'Doc says you're okay without it, but it I reckon you could do with the help. When you feel up to it, I'll get you back into bed.' She moved a chair beside him, waving his mother into it. 'Just hold his hand a bit. He'll be perking up again in a sec.'

Dan closed his eyes and sucked in oxygen. His lungs settled but his embarrassment didn't. He avoided looking at his mother, even though her hand held his, her thumb tracing a pattern across his palm. What if she asked about Felicity? Why did he let the woman's name cross his lips? Another warm flush scaled his neck making him shiver.

A coarse white blanket floated over him. Busy hands tucked it around him. Relieved his body was hidden, he relaxed. But green eyes floated before him, hands of steel pulled his head down, down… orange lips parted to engulf him. His whole body shuddered. How could he? Why hadn't he escaped? But the worst thing was… he'd wanted her. He hated her yet he'd wanted her. And Dad saw his shame. He deserved everything that happened to him. If only he'd died. Died? He thought he had died.

'Dan.'

Mum! What if she found out what happened? He wondered if he could look her in the eye ever again. He could pretend he was asleep. It had rescued him a few times when he was little.

'Dan, Rodger is here.'

Dan swallowed. *Rodger?* Could he talk to him or would he see into his confusion? He opened his eyes a little and

El Roi

lifted one hand, with tubes hanging everywhere, to his friend. 'Rodger. Good to see you.'

'It's good to see you looking so much better, mate. You sure gave me a fright.'

His mother stood. 'Take my chair, Rodger. I'm going to get a cup of tea.' She patted his hand and left.

'You've been here before?'

'Every day. Sitting. Praying. Waiting.'

'Why? How did you know I was here?'

'I found you.'

Nothing his friend said made sense. Tiredness pushed against his eyes and his back. Bed called, but he couldn't sleep now. He had to know more.

'I don't get it.'

'I found your mother, so I brought her around to visit as a Christmas surprise. Some surprise! We found you face down on the ground. Looked like you were dead.'

'I didn't see you.'

'You couldn't see anything. Your eyes were planted in the ground. You appeared lifeless.'

'But, I watched…' The scene floated before his eyes. Red curls running. His dad stopping to grab something from his back. The pain… the pain. It sliced through his heart, stabbing deeper as though someone twisted a knife.

A wail, his wail, sliced the air. Behind him, machines screeched their complaint.

'Dan. Hang on, mate. I love you. I love you.' Rodger faded away.

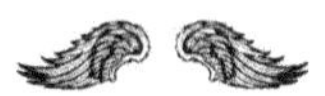

Dark. Deep and dank.

Enveloping, stifling and ugly.

He tried to run from it but it was neverending. He pushed it away but its tentacles sucked him closer. There was an answer somewhere. Something about light. Darkness couldn't put out light. But where was the light? His torch. He turned for his backpack but it wasn't on his back. He Brews. If he could just find He Brews. There was always light there. Jesus…

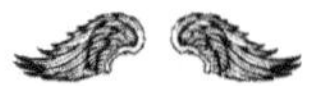

'Jesus. Come. Jesus.' Rodger was at his side, his voice quiet but firm.

Dan blinked. *Light.* Bright, invasive light. The darkness was gone.

The old-lady nurse stood where Rodger had been. 'Slow long breaths, Dan. I think you need rest.'

'No. No, must stay awake.' He couldn't sleep. The darkness was terrifying.

With a press of a button his chair started to rise. 'I'll help you to bed.'

'But… please… I must talk to Rodger.' Would he be able to stop the darkness? He had before. He knew about it. But Dan was beyond tired.

They lifted him from the chair to his bed. It was wonderful to feel the air mattress holding him, embracing him. But his limbs still shook with fear.

'Dan.' Rodger reclaimed his hand. 'You need to rest. I'm going to stay here and pray you sleep… without nightmares. When you wake and are feeling stronger, we'll talk. Now relax, sleep. Jesus is here. You are safe.'

El Roi

'But… Jesus. I'm not good enough for Jesus.'

'I know. I'm not either, but He's here anyway.'

Chapter 11

THE POLICEMAN WHO CALLED himself "Hill" sat on the straight-backed chair beside Dan's bed. A police lady leaned by the door.

'Good to see you looking so much better, Dan. You weren't good the other day.'

Dan just nodded. The coppers still made him nervous.

'Can you remember anything else to help us find your attacker, Dan?'

'Um.' Dan wished Rodger was with him but he was alone. But he was used to being alone. 'No. Can't tell you much else.'

'Your father came to visit?'

'Yeah. Picked me up and made me bring him home.'

'What did he want?'

'He said he wanted to spend Christmas with me… as if!'

'What do you think he really wanted?'

'A free place to sleep.' Dan clenched his fists as he remembered Felicity ruining his Christmas decorations, eating his food. His body stiffened. He shut his mind down.

'You fought with him?'

'Can't remember… but we always fight.'

'He makes you angry? He traps you? Takes his fists to you?'

'Not any longer.' Dan tried to corral his hatred. He pulled his 'all is okay' mask over his face. 'I escaped this time. He was going to beat the life out of me, but I ran, I got away… I thought I got away.'

'Why was he so angry?'

'Dad's always angry with me. He hates me…'

'But this time was worse. Why?'

Dan didn't know how to answer. Shame raced red up his neck. He pulled his sheet higher and closed his eyes, hoping a nurse would rush to his rescue.

The policeman waited in silence.

'Your neighbours tell us your father came, drove away and then returned. Jack watched him go into your unit and said he started yelling like a mad man. Do you know why, Dan?'

Dan searched his addled brain for a story. He was good at coming up with stories. He'd done it many times to cover for his dad, but this time he didn't have enough information… he didn't know what happened.

'What happened to my back? Do you know?'

'It appears you were stabbed in the back, or more likely someone threw a knife and it lodged in your back. But there was no knife.'

'Felicity…' Dan hoped the word didn't slip out again.

A soft hand touched his arm. He opened his eyes to see the policewoman standing beside his bed. 'Do you mind if I sit?'

He shook his head as his heart lurched.

'Tell me about Felicity, Dan. I gather this was the first time you met her?'

El Roi

He nodded and swallowed.

'We know your father married her a few weeks before Christmas. They married on the beach in Yeppoon.'

'Yeppoon?'

'It's a beach up north. The celebrant said they seemed very happy. She has curly red hair…'

'… and an orange mouth, big orange mouth.' Dan finished her sentence.

'Did she stay with you when you father left?'

Dan tried to speak but his throat was dry. He nodded his head.

The policewoman poured him a glass of water. 'She wanted to get to know you, Dan?'

The water went down the wrong passage and he choked, turning his head to the side.

When he could get his breath, the policewoman continued. 'I've researched Felicity a bit. She makes it her business to get to know young men.'

Dan swiped the water from his eyes and looked at her. 'What do you mean?'

'What did she want from you, Dan?'

'I… I…'

'So let me tell you what I think happened. She liked you and told you how spunky and strong you were …'

'She said I was sharper than Dad.'

'And somehow before you knew it, she was pressed tight against you, hugging you, and then …'

Tears came to his eyes. How embarrassing. He turned his face, wanting to run, but it still took him ages to get on his feet. And then he couldn't run.

'She trapped you in her web, didn't she? Then your father walked in and blamed you. It wasn't your fault, Dan.'

His tears escaped despite his best efforts.

'Our best guess is your father threw his knife at you and it lodged in your back. But we don't know what happened to the knife.'

'He took it with him…' His hands flew over his mouth, over his face.

'Dan. How do you know that?'

'You'll think I'm crazy.'

'Never. Not after the stories I've heard.'

'I was floating above the roof… just watching, trying to work out why my body was still down there.'

'Yes… go on.'

'Felicity ran out my door, pulling her luggage. She yelled at Dad to get another bag and the knife. Dad ran towards me. I thought he would help me, but he pulled the knife out…' He clutched his chest. The old familiar pain cramped his heart. 'He didn't care, he didn't even care…'

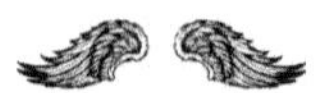

'RODGER, JESUS SAID you'd teach me about the light.' Dan had been waiting all day, hoping he could get answers to his questions.

Rodger turned, pulling the chair towards the bed. 'I'd do what?'

'Teach me about the light. You know… He is the light and in Him there is no more darkness. I never want to see darkness again.'

El Roi

Placing the chair beside Dan's recliner, Rodger raised one eyebrow. '*No More Darkness*. Reminds me of a great meal. As soon as you're well enough, I'll bring it in.'

Dan grinned. 'Sounds good but I couldn't stomach it now. But Rodger, Jesus said…'

'Hang on. What do you mean, Jesus said? Have you been talking to Him?'

'He said you were His brother. Is that right? Didn't make sense to me. But He said…'

'Dan, hold up. You're losing me. When did Jesus say I was His brother?'

'When He told me you asked Him to send me back.' An errant tear rolled down one of Dan's cheeks. He swiped away the hated sign of weakness. There was no weakness with Jesus. No. There it was… well, heavenly. Back here things were painful and confusing. Embarrassing and challenging.

'Dan.' Rodger's voice pulled him awake again. 'Dan, did you see Jesus?'

'Yeah. Haven't you?'

'Well…'

A nurse bustled down beside Dan's bed, her attention on all the gauges and dials behind him. 'Good news, Dan. Doctor says we can take a heap of these off you and then we are going to move you to a ward. Congratulations, Dan. You're being promoted!'

The clicking of switches signalled machines being switched off. She moved to the adhesive ECG dots stuck on his chest, disconnecting the leads and then removing the dots.

She turned to Rodger. 'Sorry, this will take a while. You could go and have a coffee, but it may be a couple of hours until Dan is ready for visitors.'

'I'll go, Dan, and come back later in the day. Should be at work anyway.' Rodger waved from the door.

'Wait.' Dan's hope of answers was leaving. 'But… you were going to tell me…'

The nurse moved to the other side of the bed and started working on one of the tubes.

'We'll talk later, Dan.'

'Coffee?' The very word had turned Dan's tastebuds. 'Can you bring me coffee?'

'I don't know. Nurse, can I bring him coffee?'

She waved to him. 'You sure can.'

'Rodger.'

Rodger stopped and returned to the bed. 'What's up, bro?'

'Can you bring my backpack? I think it's in the corner. It's packed.'

'Sure, buddy. If I can't get in to get it, is there something you need? Your mum brought in pyjamas and stuff.'

'I need my Bible from the backpack. But don't let Mum see it.'

The nurse started pulling the curtains. 'I need to remove the catheter.'

Rodger waved and left.

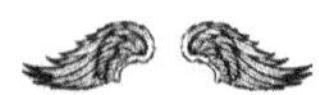

THE NOISE ASSAULTED HIM. It had from the moment they pushed him through the double doors into a normal ward.

El Roi

Nurses rushed everywhere, calling to each other and yelling at the old deaf patient.

Dan found himself one of four people in an open ward. Its walls were nearly as ugly as his walls at home. He wished they'd put him near a window, but no, he was near the passage, right opposite the desks where all the nurses and doctors gathered to talk. He was exhausted but there was too much light and noise to sleep. And he felt exposed, as though everyone in the world could walk past and peer at him. *Unsafe.* There was nothing to protect him from his dad here. If Dad found out he'd squealed on him, he was dead meat.

'Why, oh why couldn't I keep my mouth shut?' Dan didn't realise he'd spoken out loud until someone answered him.

'It's an after-effect of the anaesthetic.' Another guy whose name badge identified him as a nurse, checked his drip and held his wrist. He pulled away. 'It's ok, mate. I'm just counting your pulse rate. They've probably been doing it with machines but I prefer the human touch.' He released his hand and scribbled a number on the back of his hand. 'Your mouth can run away with you after surgery. Did you tell your girl you loved her?' He laughed and shone a torch in Dan's eyes.

'I wish!' Dan started to relax a bit. 'I told the coppers too much. If Dad finds out he'll kill me—he's already tried once.'

'That's why you're in this bed. Not the nicest view in the ward, but no one will be able to get past the nurse's station. You're a protected patient. We could enquire about witness protection, if you'd like.'

'What?'

'Sometimes we have police sitting outside rooms to make sure patients don't get attacked or attack us. Can go both ways.'

He grabbed the chart from the end of the bed and copied from his hand to the paper. He dropped onto the chair beside Dan's bed. 'I can make enquiries if you don't feel safe. Now how's your pain level? Do you need to go to the bathroom? I'll be pleased when you do.'

This guy was definitely weird. 'Why would you care?'

'Nurses always heave a sigh of relief at first wee after a catheter is removed. Means you're in good working order.'

'Nurse!' the angry call came from the opposite bed.

'Bill, you're next.' He turned to Dan. 'Sorry to yell. He's deaf. But I've got a few minutes if there's anything you need.'

'Is there anything to eat? Can I have coffee?'

'Didn't you get lunch? I'll grab some sandwiches and a coffee.'

'Don't worry about the coffee, mate. I've got one for him.' Rodger was at the door holding a coffee tray. And Dan's backpack was slung over one shoulder.

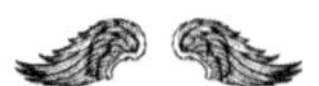

DAN REACHED TO PUT his cup on the tray. Rodger's hand grabbed it for him. Although he had been disappointed when the coffee was only a small cup, he hadn't been able to finish it. Just one sandwich had filled him. He rested his head on the back of the bed and closed his eyes. If he didn't move, he didn't hurt. It was some improvement. He heard Rodger stand and open the cupboard behind his head.

Is he leaving? Dan snapped his eyes open. 'Are you going?'

'Only if you need to sleep.'

'I can sleep all night. Can you get something out of my bag for me?'

 El Roi

Rodger pulled the bag onto the side of the bed. 'Ok. What am I looking for?'

He pulled out the big ball of clothes. 'What's this, mate?'

Dan blinked back another tear. 'Is she broken?'

Rodger carefully unwrapped the clothes, pulled out the dancing lady and passed her to Dan.

'Rose. It's Mum's Christmas present but I forgot to buy wrapping. Can you get some wrapping paper for me? I thought Felicity had broken her, but she's okay, isn't she?'

'Looks perfectly good to me. Your Mum will be in soon. She'll be mighty excited, I think.' Rodger grabbed a passing nurse. 'You don't happen to have any wrapping paper, do you?'

The nurse grinned and winked. 'We always have wrapping paper on hand.' She went to the sink in the hall and pulled out a metre or more of paper towel and laid it over the bed. 'Now all you need is tape—will red do?'

Rodger laughed and rolled the little lady over and over and around. The nurse returned and wrapped red tape around the middle and from end to end.

'A mummy for your Mummy! She's going to love this.' Rodger laid it on the bedside table and returned his attention to the bag. 'What else, Dan?'

'My Bible. It's in a plastic bag.'

Rodger dug in the bag. 'Can't see a Bible in here. How big is it?'

Dan held up two fingers. 'Bible size and it's red.'

'Hey, here's your present I gave you. You haven't opened it.'

Dan grabbed it with two hands. 'I saved it for Christmas day. Felicity fought me for it.' The flush rushed up his neck and he turned his head. Why did he have to keep saying her name?

He hated her. Hated what she'd done to him. Hated the way his body reacted every time he thought of her.

'Do you want to talk about Felicity?' Rodger's fingers rested on his arm.

Dan fingered the green ribbon on the parcel. He didn't want to talk about her. He wanted to talk about El Roi but every time he thought of Felicity, he felt guilty and as though he couldn't talk about El Roi. 'She's Dad's new wife. Marched into my place with Dad, ruined my decorations…'

'Did you tell the police about her?'

'Yes. I wish I hadn't. It was embarrassing. But they said she… she…' He turned his head away again, unable to even look at Rodger.

'Let's talk about her tomorrow. Open your present. I think you'll like it.'

Dan pulled his face back to the gift, relieved at the change of topic. He pulled at the ribbon, easing it little by little. It seemed wrong to open it when it wasn't Christmas, but he couldn't keep it for a year. The ribbon gave way and he started on the tape and stopped, risking a glance at Rodger to see if it was okay.

'Come on! Rip it open. It's been waiting for days.' Rodger laughed.

Dan ripped it off and opened a box to find a Bible. A brand new, no pages missing, Bible. He looked at Rodger. 'Mine?'

'I gave it to you, mate. Yes. It's for you.'

Dan rubbed his hands over the smooth cover. 'It's different to the one I had.'

'This one?' Rodger held up the bag with POLICE marked on it and the battered red book.

El Roi

Dan gulped. Before he could say a word, his mother rushed in the door.

'Dan, my boy. How are you? You're looking so much better. Took me an age to find you.' He accepted her kiss on his cheek but his heart went crazy. She mustn't see the evidence of his shame, a ripped drug-abused Bible. Tell-tale heat climbed his neck.

Rodger jumped to his feet and offered the lady his chair. Dan's eyes flew from side to side. What had happened to it? He couldn't see it anywhere. His gut churned. Please God don't let her see it. His mother settled into the chair and pulled out a punnet of strawberries, a bag of clothes and a packet of gum.

'Thanks, Mum. That's great.'

'And Dan has a present for you too, Mrs Furley.' Rodger picked up the package from the table. 'Freshly wrapped in the finest wrapping paper available.'

'Rodger, you shouldn't have.'

'Let me assure you I didn't. Dan bought it before his accident. I picked up his bag for him today and it was in there. Happy Christmas! Now I'm going to leave you two to chat, but, Dan, tomorrow I'll be in for a long talk.' He patted his pocket and winked. 'I'll deal with this, okay?'

Chapter 12

It was night. Outside the windows at the end of the ward, the sky was dark. But inside, in the bubble of Dan's existence, it was light. They'd turned the ward lights out and the light at the head of his bed, but there was light everywhere. Night lights, red LED lights on every powerpoint. Dan counted fourteen at the bed across from him where Bill sounded as though he was dying with every raspy breath.

A nurse had pulled the curtain between his bed and the nurses' station to lessen the light but he could still read the menu someone had dropped on his tray.

No more darkness.

This wasn't what he'd meant. The darkness he hated was the dark darkness where demons terrorised him. He closed his eyes and then screwed them tight. No hairy legs, no gross smell. In the distant recesses of his mind he remembered a black demon army and shuddered. But he couldn't bring the memory forward. It was blocked by a light.

Soft-soled shoes stopped beside his bed. 'Dan, I need to check your blood pressure again.' He turned toward the night nurse and offered his arm.

'Aren't you sleeping?' She held a contraption against his forehead.

'I think I did for a while. It's not very dark.'

'I could try and find a blindfold?' She flashed her little torch in his eyes. 'But as you're awake, can you use this machine? Inhale enough to lift the blue balls. It will help those lungs heal.'

Dan took a deep breath and blew through the plastic mouthpiece and three balls rose before the pain grabbed him and he stopped. Physiotherapy! It was more fun throwing cans at the rubbish bin at home. He lifted the balls three times before she patted his hand and told him to rest. 'Can I get you anything?'

'My backpack out of the cupboard.' He pointed and winced again. 'Please. Sorry, my manners seemed to be as weak as my lungs.'

The nurse flicked his bag on the bed and chuckled. 'Your lungs are mending well and there is nothing wrong with your manners, young man. Do you need more light?'

When he shook his head, she ruffled his blond hair, grabbed her little trolley and went to wake Bill.

The yelled response confirmed his expectation. There'd be no chance of sleeping now.

His torch was near the bottom of the bag. Delighted, he strapped it to his head, flicked the switch and placed his new Bible on his knees. It was brown. He wasn't sure he liked it but it was better than black. And not as obvious as the red. It was much bigger, but the lettering wasn't larger which didn't make much sense. Someone had written on the first page.

El Roi

Dan closed his eyes against the sting of disappointment. He thought Rodger had given him a new one, but the assumption was pretty silly. He wasn't worth a new one. Swallowing a lump in his throat, he decided to continue.

This book belongs to
Dan Furley
Presented to him by
Rodger Wellington
On *25th December 2011*

Tears ran down his cheeks. It was his. Only his. His name was in it. It wasn't second hand… but new. He turned the pages; so new they still clung together. He smelt it—a mix of leather, glue and clean. Had he ever opened a brand-new book before? He couldn't remember. His books came from the library, thumbed and stained. But this was clean and untouched and it was his.

··You are clean and untouched and you are Mine···

He spun his head, but there was no one beside him. The only voice was the nurse yelling at old Bill. But the voice, or non-voice was familiar, as though he had heard it before. He held the book to his chest and turned off his torch. Was the voice talking to him, or to the Bible? A warm cleanness spread from the centre of his being. Like warm light. Different from the light of his head lamp. A light he could feel… it reminded him of something. If only he could remember.

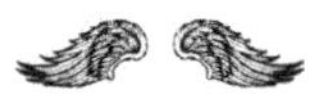

DAN BASKED IN THE WARMTH of the sun on his back. He was stuck in a wheelchair but he felt free. 'Fresh air! Real sunlight. I can't wait to get out of this place, Rodger.'

'Not long now. Will you go home?' Rodger gripped his arms around the back of the plastic chair he straddled.

'I think so. Can't really go to Mum's. She doesn't have enough room. She says she'll come every day.'

'Are you worried about being alone?'

'Nah.' Dan flicked his hair out of his eyes. 'Used to being alone. And I've got my light and…'

'And?'

'I'm hoping I'm strong enough to move my bed across the door.' Dan slammed his empty coffee cup onto the table. 'I hate this weakness. It's hard to live on the streets when you can't run.'

'You got friends who'll watch your back?'

'No. Never made friends. Too… too embarrassing. I mean they all have stuff, you know, and people and they talk about… phones… and…'

'And fathers?' Rodger barely whispered the word

'Fathers!' Dan wanted to run. Run anywhere. Just run as he'd run on the beach. But as he struggled to stand in his wheelchair, the pain stabbed him, mocking him and his weakness. His fist came down hard on the arm of the beast, the emblem of his weakness. Tears slid down his cheeks. *Can't run, can hardly walk and now tears!* He slapped his hand on the arm rests and pushed himself up. Since when did pain stop him? Since when was he such a wimp?

Rodger leapt to his side. Dan shoved him away. 'Leave me alone! I'm not an invalid.' In his mind he strode away, head

El Roi

high. In reality he crumpled, only stopping himself from falling by grabbing the back of the annoying contraption. Frustration bellowed out, causing others to stare. Soft hands were behind his back and took his weight as he fell back into the chair. His lungs burned. His breath sounded like the old geezer in the bed opposite. Holding his head in his hands he sobbed like a baby.

'Jesus, come. Jesus, come. Spirit, pour out Your oil of healing. Jesus… Jesus.'

Through his tears Dan became aware of the whispered words from Rodger. A hand touched his knee. He peered through the blond veil he was hiding behind, expecting a nurse or security guy. For a split second he saw the figure of a man. Dan flicked his hair back to look closer, but he was gone. But so was the panic, so were the tears. His hand slid to cover the spot on his knee. It was still warm. 'Rodger. Tell me about Jesus!'

Rodger talked as he pushed the chair back to the ward. Once Dan was lying on his back in bed, his pain began to ease.

'Jesus brings light. Beautiful light.'

'No more darkness?'

Rodger nodded. 'You can have Jesus with you all the time, Dan.'

'But Jesus sent me back. He said El Roi would go with me. Rodger, who is El Roi?

'Elijah? Elisha?'

'No idea who they are. I'm talking about El Roi.'

'El Shaddai?'

'No.' Dan's frustration rose again. 'He said El Roi would be with me. And He said you'd tell me.'

'The Holy Spirit is with us.'

'Jesus said El Roi.'

'When, Dan? When did you talk to Jesus?' Rodger's eyes betrayed confusion.

'You should know!' Dan threw his hands in the air. 'You're the one who sent Him.'

'I sent Him? I'm sorry, Dan, I'm not getting you at all. Tell me.'

'The demons trapped me, surrounded me, tormented me. You sent Jesus. You must know.'

Rodger frowned. They sat in silence staring at each other.

'You know, Rodg? When you asked Jesus to bring me back… that's why Jesus sent me back into this pain. I didn't want to come.' Tears flowed down Dan's cheeks again, different tears. 'The light! It was so warm, so soft, so clean. There was no darkness there…'

'Dan!' Rodger's eyes now sparkled. 'Did you meet Jesus when you died?'

'Didn't you know? He said you sent Him. He said you wanted me back.' Dan stopped and sighed.

'Tell me about the demons, Dan. Start at the beginning. I wasn't there then.'

'I was running away from Dad. Then there was this fiery pain in my back and I was on the roof looking down. I could see myself on the ground, face down. And I thought I'd escaped him. First time ever I'd got away. They reckon he threw his knife. I've seen him throw that knife. Killed the neighbour's cat from ten metres once. He could hit a target every time. I just never thought he'd….' He turned his face away from Rodger and wished again he could hide.

El Roi

Silence stretched. Dan's tears slowed.

'Tell me about the demons, Dan.' Rodger's voice was gentle but insistent.

'When Dad pulled the knife out of my back, I left. Gave in to the pull. Who wants to live after that?'

'The pull?'

'There was this force pulling me upwards. I could resist it until Dad… Anyway I was so angry, I left and then the demons started. Shoving, gloating, said they were my new family.' Dan's body started to shake.

Rodger's hand covered his. 'Sounds like hell.'

'Felt like hell. They said I'd never leave. But then…'

'Then?'

'Mum yelled. Mum called my name. The demons thought it was very funny. But then you called "Jesus". And He came.'

'The demons?'

'Don't know. The light was so bright I couldn't see anything but Him. I felt so dirty. But my clothes were clean. Then He said His brother wanted me back.'

Rodger's eyes brows jumped into his hair. 'His brother?'

'You! Don't you get it?'

'He called me His brother?' Now tears were on Rodger's cheeks. 'I'm Jesus' brother?'

Dan tried to clear his confused brain. 'Who's teaching who here?'

'You are teaching me, mate. I've never had such an experience. I've never seen Jesus.'

'You haven't? But you talk about Him as though you know Him!'

'I know Him in here.' Rodger tapped his chest.

'How?'

'His Spirit lives in me.'

'El Roi?'

'I've never known Him to be called that.'

'Well, who is He?' Dan pushed the button to lift his bed so he could see Rodger. He waited.

'Jesus is God's Son. The Holy Spirit is His Spirit. There are three parts of God, you see. When Jesus left earth, He promised to send His Spirit. He went back to the Father.'

'Father!' Dan felt his cheeks heat. 'I want Jesus, but not any Father.'

'They are a package deal, Dan.' Rodger stood. 'I've got to go. I'll leave you to think.'

El Roi

Chapter 13

THE BUZZER AT THE NURSES' station woke him. He'd ignored the first few but it had buzzed enough times to break through his slumber. A nurse ran past the desk and down the hall.

The moment the last nurse left, a wardsman, pushing a wheel chair, stopped beside his bed. 'Are you Furley?'

'No.' Dan wasn't going anywhere. He rolled over.

'Furley. Dan. It says here you need a chest X-ray before you leave tomorrow. Sorry I'm late.' He pressed the button to lower the bed. 'C'mon, Sunshine! I want to get home to bed too, you know.' He glanced over his shoulder at the empty nurses' station.

The man grabbed his feet and pulled them over the edge of the bed.

'Hey.' Dan grabbed his side. 'That hurt.'

'I've had a long day, buster. Just hop in.' The man threw a blanket at him and pushed him towards the door.

The chair moved so fast, Dan gripped the arm rest. 'Slow down, buddy.'

'You're the last. Then I'm off shift.' He spun the chair into a waiting lift.

A guy was holding a button to keep the lift doors open. As soon as the chair was in, he banged the close-door button. Dan's stomach churned as they plummeted from the tenth floor. Something wasn't right. His gut turned, and he wanted to run. But he was stuck in this stupid chair. The wardsman turned the chair towards the closed door.

'Hey. We need the third floor.' Dan had had enough X-rays to know where he was going. They sailed past floor three. The only button pressed was 'B'. 'What's going on?' His voice sounded calm but bile rose in his throat. He tried to stand but was shoved back by the wardsman.

The doors opened at the basement and he was shoved out the door. As his chair turned to the left, he saw the lift doors shut, the wardsman still inside. Who was pushing his chair? Where was the unknown person taking him? He swallowed the panic and noted everything they passed, every turn. At locked doors the person pushing him stepped in front to swipe a card. He couldn't see his face but something was very familiar about his stance. As the double glass closed behind them, it felt as though prison doors clanged shut, as though he was now on death row.

They sped through a spotless, deserted kitchen, past what looked like a room to store rubbish. A door opened in front of them and they rushed into the night.

'What's going on?' Dan steadied his voice, disguising his fear.

'We're going for a drive. There's a few people who are anxious to see you.' The voice was walking beside him. 'I'd appreciate it, if you'd cooperate. It is much easier than having to employ force.'

El Roi

'I'm not allowed to leave yet. There are other tests to happen. The doctors…'

'We decided you are well enough for our purposes.' They stopped in front of a car. The back door was open. 'Would you like to get in yourself or will I help you?'

The voice made it very clear. Dan was going with them, dead or alive. His heart pounded. He looked for a way of escape, diversion, or even delay. A hand pushed the back of his head. 'Well? Do you want me to help you?' He kneed his back through the wheelchair. Dan yelped but pulled himself up using the arm rests.

The chair was kicked away. Firm hands guided him into the back seat. The door slammed and the car crept through a maze of hospital service roads. Wheels squealed as they exited the hospital grounds and roared through deserted streets.

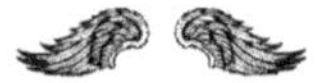

PAIN WOKE HIM. HE LAY on a thin mattress on the floor. He stretched one leg and winced as agony shot from his back and down his leg. The fog abated, banished by pain. They'd shoved a needle in his leg last night. Whatever they used had worn off.

Where was he? He had no clue. They'd changed cars twice on the way here. In the end they'd shoved him in this shed. He had a vague memory of passing a dark house. The driver's gruff voice had stirred some memory, but Dan couldn't connect anything. His desperate discomfort took all his brain energy.

The only light was a pilot light… on a power point, he assumed. Any light was better than total darkness. Moving his head around, he couldn't see even a crack of light from under a door or through a window. No cars going past. No sound except a barking dog – and it could be streets away.

Pain from his lungs throbbed through him. His breath came in short gasps. He must breathe more deeply. The physio had stressed it was the way to healing, but when he tried, a burning made him gasp. Any noise might bring his tormentor back, so he lay still, on his side, knees curled up.

The smell. That gross familiar smell. It wafted up one nostril, causing fear to shudder through his frame. Then the cackling laughter. He covered his head, but there was no safety. Even in the dark he could sense the long hairy limbs. He needed light but had nothing. No backpack. No torch.

Was he dead? Was this hell? Did hell have red pilot lights? But the agony still pulsed through him. Last time he'd left his body, the pain had stayed behind. He longed for the light of Jesus and the warm, accepting, loving hope radiating from Him. Jesus had sent him back to tell others about Him. He hadn't told anyone but Rodger—not even a nurse. Was he being punished for failing and Jesus had left him?

A tear ran down his cheek.

The demons laughed. *Jesus won't come. You're too bad. You've disobeyed Him. Failed him, missed your chance.* The mocking voices reverberated through his head.

Last time they fled when Rodger had yelled. Typical bullies. All talk and threat. But Jesus. He was beautiful. Gentle. Kind. Peaceful.

Jesus. You're beautiful. The silent thought brought peace to his brain.

 El Roi

But a counter-thought argued. *Jesus hates you. He only loves good people. You'll never be good enough for him.*

But Rodger said…

But what would Rodger know? He's a goodie goodie.

Dan jammed his hands over his ears, but the voices seemed to be inside his head.

Jesus. Are they right?

Even the thought calmed him a little. Then he remembered Rodger yelling over his dead body. Without thinking he yelled, *'Jesus!'*

It was more a whimper than a yell. He didn't have enough air to get any volume. But he sensed the demons back off a little.

'Jesus! Help!' His voice rasped but sounded a little stronger.

'As if Jesus will help you.' A voice growled from behind Dan. 'Your moaning and groaning are hard enough to sleep through, without yelling.'

A soft light lit the room. There was a bar in one corner and a few stools. The rest Dan could see was bare metal walls. He tried to turn to see who was behind him, but pain forced a moan through his mouth.

'Shut up!' A hand banged a bottle of water in front of him. 'Can you drink?'

Dan eased himself up enough to grab the water.

'Here. Take these. It's 4:30. They should stop the pain till the boss comes.' He dropped two white pills beside him.

What are they? Dan hesitated.

'I can shove them down if you like.'

Dan swallowed them. 'Who's your boss?'

'You'll find out soon enough. Now shut up and go back to sleep.' The light was gone. So were the demons. But fear clawed in his stomach. *Dad.* What would he do to him?

Deep inside, he pondered the absence of the demons. Did his whisper, 'Jesus,' rescue him from the ugly hordes? Again?

Jesus... Jesus.... Jesus. The cry remained within him. *Jesus, can You rescue me from my father?*

Would his father kill him for tattling to the police? All he'd ever wanted was a father he could talk to, go places with. A father who liked him, even. But it seemed all he had was a father determined to destroy him, first his body, then his education and now his life. Mostly he feared his evil eyes. Maybe he'd get someone else to kill him... The pain was fading...

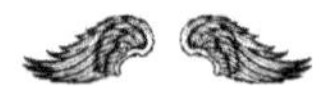

'C'MON. YOU NEED TO GET UP. Visitors coming.'

Dan moaned. He was hot, so hot. 'Water?' He gasped even to push the word out. Every movement of his chest hurt. A bottle hit the floor beside him but rolled away. He tried to reach it but fell back, panting, pain shooting through from his side to his depths. Black spots floated in front of his eyes.

'He needs a hospital.' The woman's voice sounded angry.

'I didn't ask you for an opinion. I just told you to fix him up so he can talk.' The male voice was smoother, not gruff, but familiar. Dan closed his eyes, too tired to be bothered trying to work it out.

'He needs to be lifted gently into the recliner chair. I'll need pillows, IV, saline, oxygen, antibiotics...' The voice faded away.

 El Roi

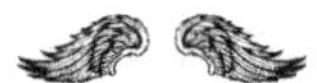

THE NEXT TIME DAN WOKE he was propped in a chair. Tubes stuck out of him in various places. An oxygen mask covered his nose and mouth. He swallowed, thirsty again. A straw was offered to him and he'd managed to draw a mouthful before it was snatched away.

'Dan. What did you tell the coppers?' A man pulled a chair up as close as he could. He leaned into Dan's face and growled the question.

Dan blinked, trying to focus. 'I… I… When? What coppers?'

'You were picked up by the boys in blue. You must've done a deal because they let you go. What did you tell them?'

'They couldn't find anything. They let me go.' Dan's brain raced but it felt like mush. It wasn't any quicker than his feet, and they were useless.

'We know you had hash. We know you got it from Fred. You were picked up and then, surprise, surprise… Fred was arrested.'

Dan looked up into dark eyes. He'd seen them before in the shed. 'Sol!'

'Have you ever heard how I deal with men who squeal to the pigs, Dan?'

'But, I didn't…'

'What else did you tell them?' Sol leapt to his feet. One hand was balled through Dan's hair, the other fist drawn back.

'Careful, Sol.' The warning came from the lady who'd offered him the drink.

With a loud curse, he dropped his fists. 'Start from the beginning. Where did the cops pick you up?'

'Near the shops. They took me back to Dad's flat. Didn't even know Dad had gone.'

'Then?'

'I told them where my flat was.'

'They searched it?'

'Yes.'

'And you reckon they found nothing.' Sol's nose was so close Dan could smell stale eggs and decay.

'A plainclothes guy chatted me up in the morning. So, I knew they were on to me. I dumped everything and cleaned the flat.'

'And didn't they ask where you got the money in your wallet?'

'I'd bought groceries and food vouchers and coins for the laundromat. They didn't ask about the thirty bucks…' Dan gasped for air. The nurse covered his face with the oxygen mask.

Sol ignored his discomfort. 'Well, who told them about Fred?'

'How would I know? I saw them take him. Heard Ginny crying.' Tears welled in his eyes. Her anguish reverberated through his brain. 'It was Christmas Eve…'

'You did tip them off then?'

'Never! I had a box of chocolates I was going to give Ginny for Christmas. I hid in the top of a tree.'

'So how did the cops know?' One bony finger, stained by cigarette smoke, poked Dan's chest.

Exhausted, Dan barely managed to lift his shoulders in a shrug.

'Did you have Fred's address in your pocket? Wallet?'

'No. Do you think I'm stupid?'

'No. But I think you're lying. I have ways of making people talk.' Sol's eyes glinted evil. He unwound his body from the chair. 'I would normally get a few tools to encourage the info

El Roi

from stubborn witnesses. But in your case, I'm going to let your own pain do the work. No more painkillers for you. I'll be back tomorrow. Then it's your choice. Tell me everything or I'll sell you to Alf.'

'Come.' He turned and grabbed the lady's arm. 'Leave him suffer.'

'But…' The lady pulled back. 'If he doesn't receive the right treatment he will lose consciousness. A dead witness isn't much use to anyone, Sol.'

The metal door banged behind them. But no lock clicked.

Chapter 14

DAN PUSHED HIS BODY UP. His back burned as though a hot rod was shoved into him. A groan burst forth and he gasped for air. His body flopped back on the chair and he grabbed the oxygen mask. *Breathe in. Breathe out.* His lungs burned. Was he going to die? He didn't mind if he went back to the Jesus light. But what about the demons? What about Amalya, his beautiful girl? Her eyes, full of joy, danced before him.

He gasped for another gasp of air and another. *Jesus.* It wasn't an audible word but a silent desperate cry from the depths of his struggle.

Jesus, why didn't You let me stay in heaven? Why send me back? Look at me. Hot tears leaked from his eyes and ran under the mask. He tried to stop them. His thirst was already dire. He needed to calm himself. In normal life he'd take a few deep breaths or run like the wind. But today he was stuck in a chair, gasping as though he'd run ten kilometres, pain slicing him in two. His mind. *Think, Dan. There has to be a way out.*

He was in a shed. It was still quite dark but bright light pushed its way past the black curtain on the single window.

He knew the door was behind him on his left and figured there would be a garage door behind him to his right. His chair faced a metal wall. A few tools were hung on the wall. What they were used for, he had no idea. Beyond them was a table or bench. Turning a little to try to see more, he felt pain shoot through him like fire. He pulled at the oxygen but the pain worsened.

All he had to do was stop breathing and he'd be with Jesus again. Of course! That was the perfect solution. He closed his mouth, held his nose and counted to keep his mind focused. His wounded lungs revolted. The little air in them added so much pressure, desperate to escape. His mouth burst open.

He couldn't move, couldn't breathe, couldn't not breathe, couldn't die. He grabbed the oxygen mask, and stayed perfectly still. And let his tears trickle down his cheeks. Real crying would hurt. Everything hurt. Heart, body and soul hurt. He hoped his father would come. He'd kill him for sure. Then it would be over.

Light! With a gentle click the door opened, brightening the shed. Dan tensed, increasing his pain. A moan slid through his lips before he could clamp down.

'Sol! Is that you, Sol?' The voice sounded nervous, unsure. 'I didn't think you'd be here, Sol. There's no car. I shouldn't have come.'

'Not Sol.' Dan hoped his hoarse whisper could be heard. Someone, anyone scared of Sol had to be a friend.

'That's my chair. What are you doing in my chair?' The voice crackled a little and moved closer but Dan still couldn't see the man.

El Roi

'Can you please help me?' Dan's whisper bought the old man to his side. His long grey whiskers hanging from his chin balanced his bald head.

Dull, confused eyes looked him up and down. 'This is my shed… well, except when Sol needs it. But his car isn't here. I saw him leave. So, I come to work. I like to work.' He shuffled past Dan and returned with a wooden kangaroo, a wonky kangaroo. He held it out. 'Skippy's not finished yet, but he's coming on.'

'He's… he's beautiful. Mate, do you have a phone?'

'One of those pesky things. Can't stand them myself but my missus says I have to carry it. She rings me when it's lunch time. I hope she's not ringing yet. I haven't even started.'

Dan tried to hold out one hand. 'My name is Dan.' He waited. The confused eyes cleared a bit and after a long wait, he thrust out an old hand, fingers twisted, veins bulging through the skin. Reaching a little further Dan grabbed it. 'I don't know your name.'

'I'm Solomon! None of those fancy shortened names for me. Sol is really Solomon the second but he won't let me call him that.'

'Solomon. What a strong name.' Dan's brain tried to climb through the pain, but as he dropped his hand a groan growled through his throat.

The old man spun and looked at Dan. The eyes opened wide and took in the tubes and the drip. 'This isn't a hospital, young man. This is my shed.' He spun around and stomped toward the door.

'Solomon! Wait. Please.'

'What?'

'I need the hospital. Can you ring the ambulance?' Dan counted his shallow breaths. *Nine, ten, eleven.* The old man had stopped but was behind Dan. *Twelve, thirteen…* His chair spun around, yanking on his driplines, sending his oxygen flying. The movement shot searing white pain from Dan's back to his chest.

'Can you use this darned thing?' An old phone was shoved in his face.

Gasping, Dan grabbed the phone. Fumbling, he dialed 000. 'Help me please…' He tried to get a decent breath. 'My name…' With effort, he focused all his strength. '… is Dan Furley.'

The phone slipped from his hand and everything faded. In his haze, he started to hallucinate.

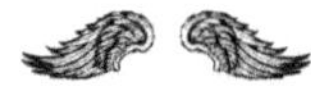

His father charged toward him. More than anger flashed in his eyes. They sparked black fury. Dan cowered, left hand over his head, right hand protected against his belly. He curled into a ball on the stone floor. There was nowhere to hide, nowhere to run.

'I'm your father! How dare you defy me? I'm your father.' The sound reverberated from the walls, echoing over and over.

Two steel-capped boots stopped near Dan's head. 'You are a no-good, pathetic, sniveling son of your rotten mother.' He cleared his throat and spat a stream of spittle on Dan's head. It ran down the back of his neck.

'You betrayed me to the kids' police at Family Services, you grabbed my woman when my back was turned and then you turned on me and blabbed to the coppers. I'm always having to

El Roi

hide. I could belt you again... but it seems that method hasn't worked. I could throw you in the river... but the coppers don't like drowned dogs polluting the waterways. You are such a shame to the Furley name, you need to be completely eliminated.'

Dan waited for the steel caps to kick him, to boot him across the stones like a football. But he was no longer sorry. He wouldn't plead. He willed himself not to cry whatever happened.

The boots walked backwards. 'Goodbye, Dan.' His laughter made Dan's skin crawl. 'Are they ready? Are they hungry?'

A voice answered from behind. 'Are you sure, Alf?'

Dan jumped to his feet. He was in a round yard, a filthy-floored round yard. There was a waterhole at one end and a gate at the other. Alf slipped through a side door and it slammed behind him.

'Now!'

Metal gates lifted and three massive crocodiles slid toward Dan, jaws snapping, tails slashing, eyes focused on their prey.

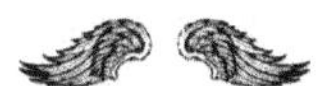

THE PAIN. THE PAIN... Dan tossed his head... too tired to open his eyes. He tried to move to ease his position.

'Hang on, young fellow. I'll help. You hurting?'

Dan recognised the voice... *but who?* His brain was so foggy... so foggy.

Again, the pain woke him. Where was he? Glimpses of an old shed, snappy crocodiles and black, angry eyes fought for space. None of it made sense.

'Dan... Can you hear me, Dan?' A hand squeezed his fingers. He tried to respond but only managed a wiggle.

'Dan, open your eyes.'

It was Rodger! His forced his eyes open and blinked against the light. The lights were dimmed and he fought to focus.

'Rodger… Where am…?'

'I'll do the talking. You listen. You rang the police. They found you in an old shed with a blubbering old man. You'd been knocked around. Lungs damaged again. Now you're in ICU.'

'Old man… shed… am I ok? Dad fed me to crocs…'

'Did you see any croc bite marks, nurse?'

A dry male voice chuckled. 'Sure did… some men think they are crocodiles.'

Dan knew his voice. 'Hey. You've nursed me before.'

'Yes… and I'm not happy. Why did you leave before you had clearance?'

'Leave?' Dan struggled to remember. 'You guys sent me to a ward. You said you'd make sure Dad couldn't get me.'

'Dan.' Rodger interrupted. 'Did your father take you?'

Dan closed his eyes to try to think. It was all so fuzzy. 'No… Sol.'

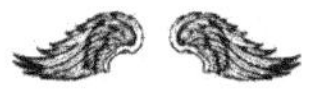

His throat was dry. His body ached. He could barely move when he woke next. The familiar beeping of machines told him he was still alive… still in ICU. He lifted one hand at least ten centimetres off the bed. It deserved an air-pump but he could only do it mentally. It reminded him of his visit to heaven. Everything seemed to happen there in the mind, not the body. Jesus knew what He'd said without him saying it aloud. Could that possibly work here?

El Roi

Rolling over his memories of his encounter with Jesus, he knew one thing. He never wanted to feel the vile guilt again. The clean washed feeling was the best. He longed for conversation with Jesus, longed to look in His face and see the love pouring from His eyes. But… Jesus wanted to introduce him to His Father. The familiar fear gurgled over his peace. But… maybe Fred… maybe if God was a Father like Fred. But Fred had betrayed his kids. On Christmas Eve of all days. Other kids had fathers who bought them computers… even cars.

He rolled the opposing ideas around and around. He wasn't getting anywhere.

'Dan.' A soft voice snatched him back to the reality of the ward. 'Are you awake? Can I take some obs?'

The smile he attempted felt lopsided. The petite little lady flashed light in his eyes and squeezed his hand. Just in time he remembered it was only a test and he squeezed back instead of yanking his hand away. He parroted his name and date of birth. She asked him what day of the week it was but he had no clue.

She laughed. 'I'm not surprised you don't know. It's Tuesday. You can tell me next time I ask.' Turning to the machines, the nurse left him in peace. He wanted to get back to the thoughts he'd had before. *Heaven. Think about Jesus and what He said. 'I'll send El Roi.' A special name. Something about seeing. That's what He'd said. So, El Roi must be somewhere close.*

'El Roi?'

'Pardon, Dan?' The nurse spun from the machines, a question in her eyes. 'I missed what you said.'

'Just talking to myself.' The heat ran up his neck. 'I'm sorry.'

She patted him on the arm. 'You're good for now. Here's the buzzer to push if you need me.' She dropped a plastic device beside him and left.

Alone, he decided to try again. 'El Roi... are You anywhere close?'

He searched the cubicle, twisting his head so his chest didn't move. But there were no white apparitions or strange men. How ridiculous. No one could get through security here. But El Roi was part of God... of course... He would slip in unseen. Dan closed his eyes. If he was unseen, there was no point looking for Him with his eyes. How had he seen Him in heaven? How did it work on earth?

Tired, his thoughts stumbled over one another. *Jesus?* Maybe that was the way... but his eyes were so heavy...

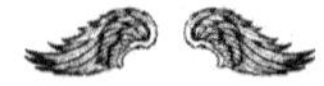

Pain woke him again but only a dull ache. He lay still, not wanting the nurse to know he was awake in case she knocked him out again.

'Dan. Can you hear me?' Same nurse. Same question.

He opened his eyes and nodded.

'How's the pain?'

'About a three or four. Much better, thanks. I need to talk to Rodger. Is he still here?'

'He's been here. Just left for a break, giving us time for me to take your obs. Then I won't need to interrupt you. What's your full name...?' And the questions were parroted again.

Rodger dropped into the chair, as soon as the nurse had finished. 'El Roi. I did some research.'

El Roi

Dan grabbed his hand. 'Tell me… quick before I go to sleep. All I seem to do is sleep.'

'And think.' Rodger grinned at him. 'Even in your sleep you are muttering about El Roi. It means *the God who sees*. It's one of many names of God. Each name tells us an aspect of his character. This one is God reassuring you He sees you all the time. There is a story about it in the Bible if you're up to it.'

Dan waved him on, hope building like a warm bubble within him.

'Abraham and his wife couldn't have children. So, Abraham slept with His wife's maid in the hope he'd have a son that way. Her name was Hagar. She fell pregnant and then gloated about it. Sarah, Abraham's wife, turned on her. Was mean and nasty. I guess domestic violence is as old as the Bible. Anyway, Hagar ran away.'

'What happened then? Did Abraham go and find her? He had made her pregnant. Shouldn't he have looked after her?'

'You'd think so… but he didn't. God sent an angel to find her in the wilderness and send her back. He also promised Ishmael, her son, would become a great nation.'

'Did she go back?'

'Yes, she did. But afterwards she had a new name for God. El Roi. It means *the God who sees me.*'

'El Roi… God sees me… Does that mean He's seen all the beatings Dad's given me, all the belittling, all the swearing?'

'Yes. He knows and he has a plan for your life.'

'That baby's father didn't even care… like my dad. Threw a knife in my back and left me to die.' Tears tunneled down Dan's cheeks. 'But Jesus rescued me and El Roi, *the God who sees me*, is with me.' He took the handful of tissues Rodger gave him and wiped his face. 'How do I talk to Him? In heaven there was no need to speak. Stuff just happened. I've got questions, you know.' Dan dried his face. He had become a real crybaby.

'Talk the same way here as you did in heaven and you'll find you'll hear the same way.' Rodger held one of Dan's hands between both of his. 'I'm going to pray using words so you can hear. Just quieten your mind and wait.'

Dan didn't hear much of the prayer. When he woke next Rodger had gone and the doctor was asking if he could examine him. 'You're improving, Dan. Is your pain easier now?'

'Much better. When can I go home?'

'When you can walk and pee. But I'll move you to a ward tonight.'

Fear snaked down his spine. 'But… what if someone comes in the night again?'

'The police have you under guard. There's been a copper at the door here since you've been in. They won't get near you again.' He raised his hand in a salute and left with his team scuttling out behind him. The nurse started removing dots and leads.

El Roi

Chapter 15

THE WARD FELT UNCOMFORTABLE… it wasn't the bed… it was the same as any other hospital bed. And they put him near a window so he could see a square of sky. At least he assumed it was sky as it was black with rays of lighter black. There were only three people in the room. Beside him was an old lady with a high-pitched voice who always wanted another cup of tea. The third person was behind a curtain. She didn't seem to speak. But the atmosphere was uncomfortable. It put him on edge as though he needed to be on guard against some vague enemy. Maybe he was just nervy. A woman in a blue uniform with a revolver strapped on her waist sat beside the main door. The only other door led to a bathroom. He should feel secure. Craning his neck as far as possible, he couldn't find anything to cause this unease.

But he couldn't see El Roi either which meant there could be other things he couldn't see. A waft of sulphur invaded his nostrils. Just like his dreams… long hairy legs, gloating ugly faces… the memories rushed back. He hadn't seen them since he died… or were they in the shed? With every nerve on edge, he waited.

Are you there, El Roi?

He'd never seen him or heard him. There must be something he'd missed. He tried to re-run his death experience. He shuddered, prickles of horror racing through his torso as the demonic hordes pushed in, claiming victory. Then the yell. Rodger's voice reaching him from earth. One word. 'Jesus!' Three words. But all the same. 'Jesus.'

The word seemed to have the same effect as light. They'd disappeared from his room when he'd turned on the light. The lights were turned off in the ward, but it didn't mean it was dark. The lights under their beds still reflected off the floor so nurses could see. Enough to stop demons showing themselves. There was no way he was closing his eyes at all. He shuddered as flashes of his nightmares invaded his memory.

A nurse, tall, round and older, stomped up to his bed with her trolley. She took a few observations. He kept his eyes closed in the hope she wouldn't talk to him. She didn't until she stood at his curtain to leave. 'Nice to have you here with us tonight, Dan. Really nice.' She chuckled—*or was it cackled?*—as she swept the curtains right around his bed. Prickles shuddered up his spine. She was terrifying. Then he realised the danger he faced wasn't a danger the policeman could protect him from… it was in another realm.

His teeth started to chatter, though he wasn't cold. His hands were clammy… his head thumping… one knee jittered. If he stilled it, the other one started. She hadn't directly threatened him, but it felt like it.

'Jesus.' The cry leaked out his mouth as a whisper. His knee stilled, his teeth quietened, as though waiting… testing. 'Jesus. The demons left when you came.' His voice was audible,

El Roi

but only just. He summoned his courage and determination. 'Jesus.' This time it was loud enough to make the lady next door snort.

His body was still, his eyes were heavy. But he dared not sleep tonight. Out of the recesses of his memory, his grandmother's voice returned.

Now I lay me down to sleep,

I pray, dear Lord, my soul to keep.

That's what he'd do. He could ask Jesus to keep his soul. Then he could sleep. Jesus would look after him. His body relaxed.

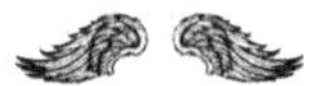

WHEN HE WOKE, THE BLACK square had turned blue and light flooded the room.

'How you doing today, Champ?' Today's nurse was tall, skinny, bearded and about forty. He felt safe.

'I've had a good sleep. Much better.'

'Great. I'll put you through the shower when I've finished doing the obs. Think you're up for it?'

Dan wriggled a bit in his bed. Enough to remind him his body still carried pain. 'I'd love a shower, but can I?'

'There are ways… pain killers first and then a shower chair. You need to start walking today anyway.'

'That's the best news I've had for days… well, except for Jesus.' Had he spoken out loud? He felt the colour warming his cheeks.

The nurse shoved the armcuff back on the stand and grinned. 'Tell me about Him when I come back for the shower. Be here soon with meds.' He flicked the curtains back and started to chat about cups of tea with the neighbouring patient.

Sniffing the air, Dan didn't smell anything except hospital smells, alcohol wipes, vague odours from the pan room, and cleaning products. A guy wiped down the bin and turned his energy to the hand basin. No sulphur. The room was peaceful this morning. Was that because he had called on Jesus, last night?

He closed his eyes and let his mind focus on the scared, retreating demons he'd seen when they encountered Jesus. A trolley squeaked into the room and a tray was plonked on his table. 'Would you like tea or coffee?' The woman chewed gum while waiting for an answer.

'Coffee, please, if I'm allowed.'

'Nothing to say you can't have it. One coffee coming up.'

His tastebuds jumped to attention at the word. He added milk and sugar and took a sip. Lukewarm and bitter. Adding all the sugar he could find, he tried again. Every tastebud drooped in disappointment. Maybe Rodger would bring a latte. Breakfast was a little better. He found he was hungry enough to eat half of everything.

After an excruciating walk to the bathroom, Dan collapsed on the shower chair and allowed the warm water to wash away the errant tears. His bearded friend, Barty, passed him shampoo and conditioner, body wash and a washer. To his relief, he could wash himself and escape further indignity like he'd tolerated in ICU.

Barty turned off the water and passed him a towel. 'So… what has Jesus done to make today good?' He took another towel and wiped Dan's feet, grinning up at him.

 El Roi

'You'll think I'm mad.'

'Try me. If I think you're mad, I'll tell you.'

Dan paused. He'd never spoken to anyone except Rodger about this stuff. But a feeling encouraged him to trust. 'The ward felt bad last night and smelled like demons. I didn't trust the nurse. Reckoned it wasn't safe to sleep.' Dan watched Barty's face, waiting for derision, but only interest showed. Maybe a bit of curiosity, or a knowing.

'But you did sleep?'

'I've learned light sends demons packing, but the other thing they are frightened of is Jesus. I called out to Jesus, so quiet no one heard, but the smell left, and I fell asleep.'

'Wow!' Barty was towelling Dan's long messy blond hair. 'Are you a Christian, mate? You must be.'

'I don't know. Still trying to work it out. I just met Jesus. It changed everything.'

'They say Jesus is the light of the world. Interesting. Those two things are what protect you from demons.' He pulled Dan's clean t-shirt over his head.

Tiredness pushed against every fibre of Dan's body. He started to shake.

'C'mon, mate. You've had enough.' He wheeled him to bed on the shower chair. 'Do you need extra painkiller?' Barty pulled up the sheet.

'I'll try not to. Can I sleep…?'

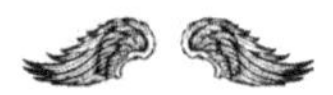

THE STRONG AROMA OF COFFEE pulled him out of slumber.

'Vanilla latte with one sugar.'

At Rodger's announcement, Dan's eyes flew open. 'Can you wind the bed up?' The coffee was magnificent. As he drank, he told Rodger about the demons leaving.

'At the name of Jesus, every knee shall bow.' Rodger grinned. 'You are winning battles, Dan. God is teaching you so much. But I just came to drop off coffee. I've got to fly now as I parked in a fifteen-minute zone. Can we talk more tonight?' He reached in Dan's cupboard and pulled out his Bible. 'Read the New Testament. God will show you.'

Barty helped him into a chair. He felt human… he still had pillows softening the sides and supporting his lungs, but his feet rested on the floor like a real person. It had never occurred to him before to be thankful for such little things. Thank You, Jesus, for my life, for rescuing me from hell and its demons. *Thank You, Jesus, for healing me, for a bath so my body is clean. Thank You, Jesus, for the sky, for a glimpse of the world beyond these walls.*

As he continued in thankfulness, the presence of God seemed to intensify, bringing a deep warmth, a soft blanket enveloping his heart. He closed his eyes and revelled in the wonder of it. It felt as if he was back in heaven.

A nurse interrupted, a different nurse. 'Sorry to disturb you, Dan. I need to grab some blood for tests.' Without waiting for permission, she started to clean his arm with an alcohol wipe.

I'm sorry, Jesus. Can You wait? Please?

Dan swallowed his disappointment, opened his eyes and smiled at the woman. She tapped the vial attached to his arm and it slowly filled with blood. 'Not the best flow, but I think I'll get enough.'

 El Roi

'I'm surprised there is any left after the amount you guys have taken.' Dan grinned. 'You're good. First try. Thank you.'

The woman pulled out the needle and pushed a cotton ball on his arm. 'All done.' She pulled his tray from his bed and lowered it so he could reach it. 'You need to drink water… as much as you can.' She filled a glass and bustled from the ward.

Taking the glass, he lifted his eyes upwards. *Thank You, Jesus for water, for the ability to drink and to eat. Thank You for coffee. Thank You for our brother who brought it for me this morning.*

His Bible was on the tray where Rodger had left it. 'Jesus, what shall I read?'

The warmth had stayed with him despite the interruption. The word that sprang to life in him was 'light'. Did his Bible have an index? He turned to the front, then the back. There. He ran his finger down a list of words. A few pages over he found it. *Light.* But instead of defining it, it gave a jumble of letters and numbers. 'Jesus, show me. I can't understand.'

Barty bustled in with another nurse. 'Meds. Can you tell me your name and date of birth?'

Dan thought of teasing him, but just parroted the information they asked for multiple times a day. He swallowed the tablets, feeling like a kid at school under the teacher's watchful eye.

'Anything else before I go, Dan?'

'Yes.'

Barty stopped at the door, and raised an eyebrow.

'Do you understand this?' Dan grabbed the Bible and pointed to the jumble of letters and numbers.

'It's a list of references of where you will find the word. See this… *Gen 1:3?* The *Gen* refers a book of the Bible, so you go to the front and find the book.' Barty flicked the pages and showed Dan how to find what he wanted.

'Wow, mate. Thanks.' Dan didn't even glance up but read the first verse. 'God said, "Let there be light." And light appeared.' With determination, he navigated the book and found the next verse, and the next. He found a menu on his table and ripped it into strips, using them to mark the passages. As he read the very last one, he found what he was looking for. *'God is light. In Him there is no darkness at all.'*

Exhausted, he lay back to rest and stretched his mind back to heaven. He couldn't see anything but light… not even any shadows in the background. Everything was bright.

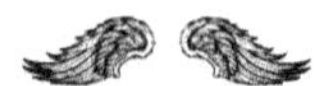

He was pulled out of a deep sleep by his physiotherapist. 'Oh, my personal torturer has returned.'

The young woman laughed. 'I guess you are just lucky, Dan.'

Every minute he could salvage between hospital interruptions, he returned to his Bible and followed his search. He started marking words and underlining sentences. At first, he felt guilty and then remembered he owned this book. Would Rodger think he defaced it? But once started, he even made notes in the margin. He needed a notebook, but couldn't figure out how to get one. Instead, he asked Barty for some hand towel. The nurses took notes on it all the time. It worked like a notebook, if he remembered to number the pages… or rather... sheets.

El Roi

Barty skidded to a stop by his bed. 'I'm finished for the day. Is there anything I can help you with before I go?'

Dan stuck his hand out. 'Thanks for being a mate as well as my nurse.'

Barty shook his hand. 'I'll be back in the morning.' He turned to go and stopped, returning as though doing an observation again. While near his ear, he whispered. 'Keep your notes out of sight tonight. Wanda is back. She reacts to anything that smells like a Bible.' He straightened up, waved and was gone.

The sulphury smell wafted into the ward ahead of her. Dan shrugged. It didn't make any difference. He just had to fight against the demons for safety and sleep. *Jesus.* The name was becoming the most necessary thing for his survival. It felt as though there were more people than Dad who wanted him dead.

His mother came in after work. She had more clothes for him, and a Coke and his favourite chocolate. She busied herself tidying the cupboard and the drawer. 'What is this? Looks like nurse's scribble.'

As she moved to the bin, he yelled. 'Mum. They are my notes. Please put them in my Bible.'

'Bible?' She stopped halfway to the bin, peering at the paper towel as though it was contaminated.

'I had nothing to write on, so I used what the nurses use.'

Dan watched her trying to understand. Slowly she turned and put the notes safe in his Bible. 'You interested in the Bible? My mum would've been pleased.'

'I'm interested in Jesus. The Bible tells me about Him.' He waited, watching his mum fussing about the room. 'I met Him.'

'You met who?'

'Jesus.'

'How? You can't meet Jesus.' She stopped her fussing and stared at him. 'Jesus went to heaven.'

'That's where I met Him.'

'Dan, don't be ridiculous. You're a good boy, but not good enough to get to heaven.'

'You're right. I was on my way to hell. It was terrifying. Then you came with Rodger, remember.'

She sat heavily in the chair. 'Are you talking about the night you were stabbed?' At his nod, tears shone in her eyes. 'I thought you were dead; thought I'd lost you.'

'I was. Can I tell you about it?' Dan was interrupted by the tall, gruff nurse who wanted to take his temperature. She bustled around, pushing past Dan's mum, who rose from the chair and looked to escape out the door.

Dan grabbed her hand. 'Don't go, Mum. I want to tell you about meeting Jesus.'

The nurse turned on him, fire in her eyes. 'Don't swear in my ward, young man.'

Turning his eyes fully onto her, still holding his mother's hand, he said, 'I wasn't swearing. I was just talking about meeting Jesus. Would you like to hear the story? Jesus is just so beautiful.'

The nurse spun around and fled.

Dan grinned at his mother. 'She's scared of Jesus. There's lots of demons with her and they hate Jesus.'

El Roi

His mother grabbed her bag. 'I have to go. I'll try and get back tomorrow.' She was nearly out the door when she remembered to return and kiss him on the cheek. He could hear her heels clanking down the corridor as though the devil was on her tail.

Jesus, Jesus... Dan lay his bed back and closed his eyes. Heavy tiredness pushed on his eyes, but his heart buzzed, excited. He was tempted to doze, but what if the nurse came back?

Jesus, how do I keep you here?

···I'll never leave you···

But what if I do something wrong? I'm not pure, you know.

···I washed you clean···

That's true... in heaven I was clean... everything is clean there...

···You are still clean···

Can I go back to heaven?

···Who would tell your mum then? So many need to know about Jesus···

Aren't you Jesus?

···I'm El Roi. I'm Jesus' friend, your comforter···

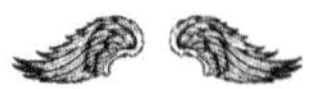

DINNER WAS DELICIOUS... or maybe his appetite was returning. In the bathroom, washing his hands, he caught sight of a ragged, pale individual in the mirror. Asking for his hairbrush, he sat in bed and pulled it though his hair. He needed a haircut or more conditioner.

···The red shirt will help···

El Roi. Is that your idea or mine?

···I've got a surprise for you···

A nurse stopped to check his blood pressure, so he asked her to help him put on his red shirt. Seemed crazy. It was only Rodger coming. He refused the nurse's offer to sit him in the chair. His body ached. He settled back on his pillows and pondered El Roi. Unseen, unfelt but somehow there.

El Roi

<h1 style="text-align:center">Chapter 16</h1>

'DAN?'

At the soft voice, his eyes flew open. 'Amalya!' His heart beat a crazy dance. 'How? Is it really you?'

She grinned, threw her long chocolate hair over her shoulder, walked right up to him and kissed his cheek. Maybe heaven had come to him. He grabbed her hand and grinned like a fool.

'I just came back from holidays. At church, Rodger was thanking everyone for praying for Dan. I didn't realise it was you until one of the kids from the train told me. I checked with Rodger. He told me how to find you.'

He squeezed her hand and shut his eyes tightly to try to contain the tears, but they leaked out anyway. He must say something but his throat closed on any normal words. All he could think of was how beautiful she was, sitting beside him.

She chatted to him, as though she knew he needed time. Her Christmas was full of presents, people and food. To his surprise, he wasn't jealous.

'Tell me about your Christmas, Dan. Did you go away?'

'I spent Christmas in ICU, but I went to heaven on Christmas Eve.'

Her green eyes filled with tears. 'ICU? I didn't hear that. Heaven? Did you nearly die?'

He rubbed her hand between his two. How much should he tell her? What if she ran like his mum?

…I brought her. Trust Me…

'I actually did die. I was falling into hell, gross gloating demons surrounding me… but then Rodger found my body and started yelling, "Jesus."'

Her eyes were wide deep pools of green water. She swallowed but one tear ran down her cheek. He managed to reach over far enough to catch it on one finger. He wanted to bottle it, but instead wiped it on his red shirt, near his heart.

'Go on…' Her broken whisper encouraged him.

'All of a sudden, the demons fell away, screeching… and I stood in front of this person, this beautiful shining being. I fell face down. I felt so dirty… I have done so much wrong… but it was all forgiven. Jesus made me as pure as Him. Can you believe it?'

Tears flowed down her face. Was she horrified at his confession? Would she leave?

Looking for tissues, she gave up and wiped her face on his sheet. 'And then?'

'We talked for a bit and then He said Rodger had asked for me to go back. He wanted to know if I'd return and tell people about Him. I agreed and in an instant I'm back on earth in dreadful pain.'

'What… what does it feel like to be forgiven?'

El Roi

'Amazing… light… hopeful… clean. But the best thing is Jesus.'

'Jesus?'

'I've only got to say His name and any demons plaguing me back off, scared. Before I had to leave the light on all night.'

'Dan… How awful and wonderful and amazing. I've never heard a story like it before.'

'I should be dead, Amalya. But I've been given another chance. I've just one thing I need to sort out. It seems Jesus comes in a package with a Father called God. I don't want anything to do with any father. Rodger says God's a good father… but it's hard for me to believe.'

'Dan.' Green eyes stared at him, confused. 'Of course, God is a good father. Why wouldn't he be?'

'My experience of a father probably skews my view. I'm terrified of my dad. Did you see the policeman at the door?'

'Yes.'

'There to protect me from my dad.'

'But, why?'

'Dad threw a knife at my back. Then pulled it back out and left me face down in the dirt. Now I'm a witness. Better for Dad if I was dead.' He took a deep breath. What was he thinking, unloading all his pain on her? She'd run for good now. He couldn't even lift his eyes to see her reaction. Finger by finger, he forced his hand open so she could leave. 'Amalya. I'm so sorry. I shouldn't have dumped on you like that. I guess you won't want to hang around a loser like me any longer.' His last finger was open. All five of her fingers curled around his hand. He was a coward… couldn't lift his eyes. To his horror, tears escaped. Only a couple trickled down before he closed them off… he'd had plenty of practice at making tears run inside.

Getting off her chair she sat on the bed, right beside him. Then her head was on his shoulder and her tears soaked into his red shirt. His heart galloped but his arm curled around her and held her. Would it be the only chance he ever had to hold this amazing woman? In this position, he was very aware she wasn't a girl. She was all woman, and the only woman he would ever want.

'Dan… ' She lifted her head and looked into his lowered eyes. 'That's one of the most amazing things that's happened to me.'

'I don't understand.' Now she had his eyes, he couldn't pull them off hers. Hers shone at him, wet, wide and sincere.

'You just trusted me enough to tell of your greatest heartbreak. My heart is so sad for what you've suffered… but it's so excited as well because you shared your pain with me.'

He had no words. He pulled her head back down onto his shoulder, his fingers in her silky hair, her scent invading his nostrils and waited for his heart to settle… though he wanted to wait forever.

'Milly.' The deep male voice from the doorway pulled both their heads up.

'Daddy. Come in and meet Dan.' Milly showed no sign of the panic that coursed through Dan. Her father! What would he do to him for touching his daughter?

'Dan. This is my dad, John. Daddy, please sit down. Dan has just been telling me what happened to him.'

Palpitations coursed through his body as John sat and listened to Milly. Dan knew he was a sitting duck. Stuck in a

El Roi

hospital bed. No way to defend himself… but John's body was relaxed, his eyes were caring and full of love for his daughter. Amazed, Dan watched their conversation and his body relaxed a little.

When visiting time was over, John stood and held out his hand. Dan took it and nothing was said but a mutual admiration formed in the shake. Amalya leaned over and kissed Dan's cheek, in front of her father. 'I'll be back soon, Dan.' She got to the door and stopped. 'Could I have your number? So I can text you.'

Heat flared up his neck and onto his face. 'I… I don't have a phone. I was supposed to work all holidays to get one and a laptop…' He shrugged. 'I'm sorry, Amalya.'

She turned and came back. 'There's no shame in not having a phone. It was rude of me to assume.' She kissed his cheek again and rushed after her father.

His hand covered the double-kissed spot, as though to hold them in place. And for reasons he couldn't fathom, he cried.

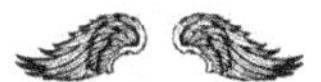

It was dark… well, as dark as a hospital can be. Dan was woken by the giant nurse hovering… standing… looking. Her stare must have woken him, or was it El Roi? He didn't stir but, like a lion eyeing his prey, he lay quiet, still, breathing deeply. He watched through hooded eyes as she glanced this way and the other. She went to the door and checked the corridor, turned and marched toward him as though she had reached a decision.

'Have you come to hear more about Jesus?' Dan kept his voice soft but firm. It startled her. Pulled her up in mid-stride.

'Don't mention that name in my ward.' She snarled, advancing, but not as confident as she had been.

'Jesus… He's my friend, you know. I met Him in heaven. Jesus saved me from hordes of demons. They fled when He came.'

She fled.

Thanks, Jesus. But what does she want with me?

…The enemy doesn't like losing. He lost you. Be on guard…

But I can't stop the enemy coming. I've tried. But… light and the word 'Jesus' seems to scare them.

…You're learning fast…

Will I always have to fight?

…No. Your resistance makes the enemy flee. Like your nurse…

Jesus, You're amazing. I want to walk with You forever.

…I want to walk in you forever…

I… I think I'm ready to meet the Father, now. I mean John seemed to be an amazing father… so I figure Your Father must be amazing.

…He's right here with Me and El Roi. He's so pleased with you…

A hug seemed to envelope Dan. Like arms of warm oil encasing his whole body, it flowed through his being, enveloped his mind… Overcome, he rested… too overwhelmed to even respond.

Next morning, Dan wondered if it had been a dream. But he was indefinably different. And stronger. He pulled himself out of bed and shuffled to the bathroom before Barty came in to help. Lightness flowed through him… less weight, less darkness… not enough to dance to the tattoo beating in his heart, but enough to release laughter… and singing… and joy.

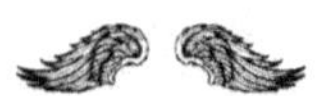

 El Roi

Two days later Rodger picked him up and drove him home. Farewelling his wheelchair, he walked to the car. Not completely upright, still aching when he moved, but he could move. He felt free and excited.

'I hear you turned down John's offer of staying with them for a while.' Rodger shoved his key in the ignition.

'He has been so kind… but I can look after myself, providing you or Mum shop for my food. It will be good to be home. And I don't want Amalya to feel as though she's obliged to nurse me.'

In front of the flats, he swung open the car door and levered himself out. Halfway down the path, his eyes fell on the spot where he had fallen face down, the place of his father's betrayal. Like a mini-movie he watched his father yank out the knife and run away. His feet stilled of their own accord and one hand started to shake.

Rodger's hand grabbed his elbow. 'Memories not so good?'

Jesus… how do I navigate this path? How do I walk it every day?

· · · Forgive · · ·

Forgive?

· · · Forgive your father for betraying you · · ·

But El Roi… how can I?

· · · Just say the words… make the decision and allow Jesus to make the words real · · ·

He took a few more shaky steps and stopped. 'I forgive Dad.' It was a whisper.

'Did you say something, Dan?'

He screwed up his eyes against the dreadful pain in his chest. The daggers of rejection were more painful than the knife in his back. He gasped, trying to suck air back into his lungs.

···Louder···

···And in My name···

The thought was soft but clear. Hanging on to Rodger's arm, he stood as tall as he could and planted his feet on the path. 'In Jesus' name, I forgive you, Dad, as Jesus has forgiven me. I have a new Father, a Father in heaven who loves me.' Once again, the annoying tears escaped.

···Cleansing tears. Who else?···

He took a deep breath. 'In Jesus' name, I forgive Felicity. You have no hold on me.' He swiped away the last of his tears and stepped over the memory and marched down to his door.

Rodger unlocked the new deadlock and pushed open the door. His room was clean and tidy. Mum must have been here. There was food, all his favorites, and dinner waiting to be heated.

Sinking onto the closest chair, he breathed in the clean, non-hospital smell. Rodger dropped his backpack near his bed and took the other chair.

'Such bravery, Dan. To step over offence, literally, is amazing.'

'It was hard… but that's what El Roi said to do… and now the memory doesn't hurt like it did. It's like I'm forgiven again. Free.'

'Forgiveness. It's another thing the enemy flees from.'

Dan grinned. 'Seems all I have to do is listen to the voice of El Roi.'

 El Roi

Rodger nodded and handed him a bag. 'John sent this for you.'

Raising his eyebrows, Dan took the bag. 'He didn't have to.' Opening it, his eyebrows shot into his hairline. He pulled out a smartphone box. 'What? Rodger, what is this?'

'He said to tell you… it is one of their old ones they've replaced, and it was sitting unused in the cupboard. He has connected it to the network for you. You will have to top up the sim card each month. He will help you to do that. Go on, open it.'

Within seconds, Dan learned how to use a phone. Two people were already in the contact list. John and Amalya. Rodger showed him how to add others by adding his own number and Dan's mother's.

'How do I send a text?'

When he pressed the SEND button on his first text to Amalya, his heart danced. What a miracle. He could contact her every day.

Rodger dropped his hand on Dan's shoulder. 'You settle in. I'm only a phone call away. Is there anything else I can help you with before I go?'

'Pray?'

'Father, I thank You for the new life You have given Dan. I thank You for the special work You have done in his heart. Please send Your angels to surround his home to protect him.' Rodger hugged Dan and turned to the door. 'I don't like leaving you by yourself, but I guess you are used to it.'

'I've been by myself a lot, but I will never be alone again. My special friend, El Roi, is right here.' He tapped his heart and grinned.

Epilogue

As Dan walked off the graduation stage, Amalya ran to him, throwing her arms around his neck. 'How very exciting! Engineer Dan Furley.'

Dan squeezed her and grinned. 'I would never have managed it without you.'

'Rubbish.' Her eyes danced in rhythm with her feet as she held his hand. 'Your determination has always been your driving force.'

Amalya's parents and his mum joined the celebration. He hugged each one of them, grateful for their encouragement and help. His father was still in jail. Although he'd visited him several times, their relationship was very strained.

Grinning at the group, he apologised. 'I've got to say goodbye to a couple of people. Can we meet you at the restaurant?'

A hand slapped him on the back. He spun and engulfed Rodger in a huge hug, lifting him off the ground. 'My man-angel. Thank you.'

Curling his fingers around Amalya's hand, he led her to farewell his friends. Then they found his old Corolla in the crowded carpark. As he opened the door for her to get in, his news bubbled out of his mouth. 'I got the permanent job. Out of all of us, they chose me to stay after the internship. I start after Christmas.'

He rushed around to the driver's door.

'Dan. How wonderful!'

He started the car and pulled out into the traffic.

'Wait, Dan! You're going the wrong way. Mum and Dad are waiting…'

'I've got something to show you first.' He drove on for half a minute before pulling his wheel towards the kerb and parking the car. 'Won't take long.'

As he opened her door, his heart danced a crazy tattoo in his chest. Together they ran across the lawn to their special spot near the pond. They'd often met there, studied there, kissed there.

He couldn't wait another minute. Years and years he'd held his tongue. He skidded onto his knees before she could sit on their bench. 'Amalya… please, will you marry me? I love you so much, I can't wait another minute to know you will always be with me.'

Throwing her arms around him, she nodded and laughed and kissed him. Then he remembered and dug in his pants to pull out the ring. As he pushed it on her finger and wiped away her tears with his kisses, his heart did cartwheels.

'There is just one thing.' Pulling his head back, his eyes sought hers and held them. 'I think they are going to ask me

El Roi

to work in Wambaroo. Can you come with me? I can't bear to be separated from you.'

'I love Wamberoo… ocean… bush… How long till it happens?'

'Six weeks… about?' He held his breath, hoping against hope.

'Six weeks!' She spun around. 'Come on, handsome. Take me to our mothers. There's lots of work to do.'

Confused he shook his head. 'Is that a no or a yes?'

Grabbing his hand, she dragged him to the car. 'Yes, of course. Which date?'

Running now, he passed her to open her door.

She blew him a kiss. *Engineer and Mrs D Furley.* I've been practising saying that for ages.'

In front of the car, he jumped and clicked his heels together. He threw a kiss heavenward to his grandmother who had taught him to dream. Lifting his arm, he saluted his team in heaven.

Father God, You have blessed me beyond measure. I love You.

···It's My pleasure to give good gifts to My children. I love you too, Dan···

Author's Note

I HOPE YOU ENJOYED walking with Dan. At many spots in this story, I had to pause and wait for the Holy Spirit's leading to know where the story would head next. I'm really just His tool and I enjoyed the unfolding of the book.

If you haven't read *El Shaddai*, it continues Dan and Milly's adventures with God. I'm currently working on other books in this series so there more stories are coming that explore their lives as they are led by Holy Spirit.

If you want books or just to chat you can find me on Facebook or email me at

jowanmer@gmail.com

About Jo Wanmer

JO LIVES IN MORETON BAY CITY, an emerging community north of Brisbane. She has always been a Queenslander. She and her husband Steve live busy lives filled with God, business and family. Their family has grown astronomically, now embracing eleven beautiful great-grand children who fill their home and garden with noise and laughter.

Jo never imagined herself as a writer, but God moved so graciously during years of family trauma that she wrote her first book to tell what He had done. Though the Bud be Bruised won a CALEB award and was published twelve years ago. Encouraged, she found a love of writing stories, especially stories that bring a message of hope and redemption. Many of her short stories are published in anthologies, but twelve years passed before this, her next novel was published.

El Shaddai is the first of a series of titles, four of which are written. You can follow their progress on

www.jowanmer.com.au

or her Author page on Facebook:

https://www.facebook.com/profile.php?id=100066475044806

Though the Bud be Bruised and *El Shaddai* can be found on Amazon or you can order direct from the author:

jowanmer@gmail.com

www.ingramcontent.com/pod-product-compliance
Lightning Source LLC
Chambersburg PA
CBHW070948190726
48292CB00004B/1375